S70

SCIENCE FI
ALLEN COUNTY PUBLIC LIB

P9-EEI-875

ACPL ITEM
DISCARDED

The Dagda repeated, almost chant-ing ritually, "This is a picture of Earth." Giles was suddenly dizzy and the map swam before him. Earth—the magic, mystic, forbid-den word—and the Dagda said it so freely. Earth . . .

Only hours before, Giles had truly believed that there was no Earth—that it was only the wild dream of a few fanatics. Even as he walked through the streets of Niflhel, his shoes crunching against the layer of soot that carpeted the walks, he believed it—just as he was taught, just as he had vowed.

This is madness, he thought. There is no Earth. Perhaps he should forget it and go home. Still, he continued, not really knowing why.

When he reached his destina-tion, Giles looked up through the haze. The red glow from the east-ern factories lit the night sky like an inferno, and his eyes burned

(Continued on back flap)

(Continued from front flap)

from the particles of grit that filled the air. There, shining dimly in the second floor window, was the small, green translucent sphere—the object he had been told to look for. Giles entered the dark doorway and ascended the stairs, nervously anticipating his first meeting with the Earth Worshippers.

Legend of Lost Earth shows how Earth herself reaches a solution to man's ultimate greed, ambition, oppression, and corruption. It is a gripping novel, on one level supported by scientific theory, and on another, subject to a multitude of interpretations—the mark of truly great science fiction.

LEGEND OF LOST EARTH

By the same author

Liza
Home to Hawaii
Why Not Join the Giraffes?
Meanwhile, Back at the Castle
No More Trains to Tottenville
There's a Pizza Back in Cleveland
  (*with Mary Anderson*)
Peter's Angel: A Story about Monsters

LEGEND OF LOST EARTH

by Hope Campbell

Four Winds Press   New York

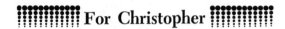 For Christopher

LIBRARY OF CONGRESS CATALOGING IN PUBLICATION DATA

Campbell, Hope.
　Legend of lost earth.

　SUMMARY: Nineteen-year-old Giles, a model citizen of Niflhel, be-
comes involved with members of an illegal society that believes Earth
truly existed.
　[1. Science fiction]　I. Title.
PZ7.C15414Le4　　[Fic]　　　76–48079
ISBN　0–590–07397–4

Published by Four Winds Press
A division of Scholastic Magazines, Inc., New York, N.Y.
Copyright © 1977, 1963 by Geraldine Wallis

All rights reserved
Printed in the United States of America
Library of Congress Catalog Card Number: 76–48079

1 2 3 4 5　81 80 79 78 77

AUTHOR'S NOTE

I wish to gratefully acknowledge the translators and publishers of the various Celtic works and Scottish runes from which I have drawn. 1949110

The translation of a part of "The Phoenix" from *The Poems Of Cynewulf* is by Charles W. Kennedy, published by E. P. Dutton & Co., New York, and Routledge & Kegan Paul Ltd., London.

"The Rune of the Peat Fire" and "A Highland Invocation for Protection" from *Carmina Gadelica* were translated by Alexander Charmichael, published by Oliver & Boyd Ltd., London.

"A Rune used by the Islanders of Aran in Galway asking the Protection of Mary and Brigit" from *The Religious Songs of Connacht* was translated by Douglas Hyde, originally published by Ernest Benn Limited, London; also found in Margaret Cushing Osgood's anthology of poetry, *The City Without Walls,* published by Macmillan.

"The Mystery of Amergin" or "The Song of Amergin" appears in various works: in *Celtic Literatures* by William Sharp and Ernest Rhys; in *Lyra Celtica,* translated by Elizabeth A. Sharp; in *The White Goddess* by Robert Graves, translated by John MacNeill.

"The Seven Questions put by Catwg the Wise" is also from *Lyra Celtica,* originally published by J. Grant, Edinburgh.

▓▓▓▓▓ ONE ▓▓▓▓▓

It was night in Niflhel.

Giles Chulainn stared down at the pavement, trying not to look up as he walked through the streets of the city. Still, it was impossible to escape the pervasive smoke that hung like a heavy cloud over the low, black buildings. His feet made crunching noises as they ground into the layer of soot that carpeted the walks. Sometimes it wasn't this bad—sometimes the mixture of dirt and soot was like a blanket of fine ash that curled up in small puffs and vanished as one walked along. Tonight the red glow from the eastern factories lit the sky like an inferno and particles of grit floated through the streets, burning and stinging his eyes. Giles hated the nighttime. It was worse than the days of Niflhel, even more somber and depressing.

He stopped walking for a moment and blinked through the haze. There weren't many people about. Most of them would have—sensibly—taken the Underground directly home to the periphery of the city and avoided being caught in this rain of industrial waste.

Momentarily he considered doing the same. His inten-
tion of how to spend the evening was the maddest
scheme that had occurred to him in all his eighteen
years. Perhaps he should forget it and go home.

But the picture of home that rose before him was as
bleak and depressing as the streets of Niflhel. A squat
hut, among thousands of others, arranged in undeviat-
ing, symmetrical rows, only broken here and there by
the tall, gaunt elevator shafts that rose from the Underground . . . no, he wouldn't go home.

He looked at the street number and turned into a
smaller lane. His cape flapped behind him in a sudden
gust of wind and an eddy of soot blew into his eyes.
Giles pulled his visor down and drew the black cape
and hood more closely around him. The building should
be nearby. He peered up at the grilled back windows
that lined the alley. Why did he have to come in
through the rear? Why all the secrecy about this meeting? Or this madness, a part of him said.

There was an echo of footsteps from behind. Giles
whirled and ducked into a doorway, flattening himself
against the side. Two hooded figures walked slowly and
silently past, not glancing in his direction. He watched
as they strolled in the same measured pace several yards
ahead. Then they turned and disappeared. Giles choked,
breathing deeply, amazed at his own furtiveness and
fear. These groups were all right—it wasn't Contrary to
attend—so why this sudden lurch in the pit of his
stomach?

He himself had called it "madness" a moment ago—
also he didn't know anyone who had ever actually attended. It must be just the newness and the strange-

ness, then. He stared ahead to the spot where the two figures had disappeared and slowly walked on.

A green light. A round, green light shining in a second-story loft in store number 63, about halfway down the building compound. A dim green light shaped like a ball. "And when you see it," the girl had said, "ascend the stairway quietly, please. We have no wish for advertisement."

He saw the translucent green sphere ahead, glowing faintly, and it gave him an eerie sensation. He had an uncomfortable desire to turn back. Instead he entered the dark doorway and climbed the stairs to the second floor. There he stopped, annoyed to find that he was now extremely nervous.

One door along the hallway was slightly ajar and Giles cautiously pushed it open. He found the shower room with a series of cubicles from which came the sound of air jets. He removed his cape, hung it on a wall hook, and stepped into one of the open cubicles. The doors sealed behind him, and inside the air vacuum was strong. He felt relieved when the last particle of soot was sucked from his clothes and hair and face and hands. Now he could breathe more freely and some of the tension left him.

When he stepped out there were three other people in the room—and one of them was the girl! He hardly had eyes for the others, noting only that they were men about his age. He looked at the girl.

This morning she had been too quick for him. She appeared beside him on the Underground so abruptly that he'd been taken by surprise. With a strange urgency she had whispered to him of this meeting. But before

3

he had a chance to even consider his reaction, she had disappeared. For a moment Giles had wondered if she'd been there—if she weren't an apparition.

She was real enough, now that he saw her clearly. Her hair was a deep, midnight black; her eyes were a similar shape and color as his own, although hers were greener and more brilliant. There was an odd light in them. Her arms were pale and faintly freckled, as were his—usually a sure sign of family connection. She might be a member of his own family branch. . . .

"Are you from the Chulainns?" he asked her, heedless of the others.

The two men looked at him in surprise. The girl just stared at him—oddly, Giles thought—and without answering entered a shower cubicle. Giles looked at the others, smiled and shrugged. They didn't respond. Their faces remained expressionless as they turned and left the room.

He stared after them, nervous and uneasy again. Who *were* these people who displayed none of the social mannerisms of Niflhel? What was he getting into? He must be crazy to come here! Just because a girl, who now didn't seem or want to recognize him, had whispered in his ear. Once again he reconsidered. But leaving now would be as embarrassing as staying.

He stepped out of the shower room to the hall where the green light shimmered faintly from under another door. Giles paused for a moment and then gingerly turned the handle.

The green light seemed to fill the room. Actually it came only from the round green globe that hung before the window. But there was no other illumination, so

4

the effect was like being plunged into a limpid green sea. Giles caught his breath. There was something startling in the impression of that green light, so different from the murky black buildings of Niflhel, and the dark, overcast, sometimes humid, red sky. It was like balm, so unexpectedly soothing that he felt the shock through his whole body. So this is why people come here, he thought. That was his first impression.

The room itself was nothing but a long bare loft filled with rows of seats and people patiently waiting. Or were they just waiting? There was another quality present. Giles had the distinct sensation that these people were doing something—but what it was he couldn't tell. He found a seat near the rear and sat down to scan the faces around him. Surprisingly he saw that many were from the city's top strata. They weren't all of his age, some were past middle-age or even old. All were quiet and seemed to have their attention fixed on the green globe. Nobody returned his glance. Giles looked at it, too, narrowing his eyes as he tried to see what the others were seeing. But he saw nothing except the formation of a halo if he stared hard enough.

All of a sudden the whole thing struck him as being extraordinarily silly and he had a wild impulse to laugh —at himself as much as anything else. What did he imagine he was doing here!

A man walked from the back of the room up one of the side aisles and turned to face them. Giles had never seen him before, but the man's face startled him, and removed all his feelings of humor. Surely this was one of the Dagdas, the oldest and most venerated branch of Giles's own family. A remote branch, to be sure, yet a

5

strain that all the Chulainns regarded with great respect. And this man must be one of the oldest—perhaps the oldest—of the Dagdas, Giles decided, studying him carefully. He wasted no time on preliminaries, but jumped to the heart of what Giles, at least, had been experiencing.

"Of course, there's no mystery in why you all feel more tranquil here. We have very little green in Niflhel and what there is of it is chemically produced. So is the globe. But the meaning behind the globe attracts you emotionally and therefore the color has a soothing effect." He stopped, and seemed to be weighing something before he went on. Then his voice changed from a tone of having said all this hundreds of times before, to one of anger and immediacy.

"A lot of people come here just for that. For this 'sense of peace' or whatever it is they think they receive from staring at this globe, which is nothing more than self-hypnosis. For a long time we didn't mind *how* people came here as long as they came. We wished only to keep the idea alive in as many hearts as possible."

Giles winced at the words, even if the man was a Dagda.

"However, the situation is now different. Our ideas have been so thoroughly despised by the Hierarchy, our groups have been so effectively eliminated by mass psychological pressure, that I feel it only fair to warn you. It is only a matter of time before we will be Classified as Contrary."

There was a chorus of gasps from a group of women sitting together. The Dagda looked at them coldly and continued without changing tone. "There is no longer room for those who aren't serious. Consequences will fall on those attending these meetings who are unlucky enough to be found out. I strongly advise most of you to regard this as your last meeting." He walked to a desk along one wall of the room and began looking through some papers.

Was he giving everyone time to digest this information? Giles watched him, fascinated. Until now he'd had no idea that Classification might be imminent. He might be putting himself in some danger by coming here. But the information now made him glad he'd come. He might never have an opportunity to witness another meeting. And regardless of the idea behind all this, there was something about that man. . . .

The Dagda reached for a large frame that was leaning against the wall beside the desk and a man in the front row jumped up to help him. Together they moved it to the center of the room in front of, and just below, the green globe. The man, who seemed to be an assistant, sat down, and the Dagda stood to one side of the frame. It contained a map of some sort and the Dagda looked at it as if he, too, were seeing it for the first time.

He said, very softly, "This is a picture of Tir na nOc . . . or, if you prefer, and as some have called it, this is a map of Earth."

Giles felt a constriction in his chest as he heard the word. That forbidden word that nevertheless lived in him, as it did in most citizens of Niflhel, in some obscure chamber of his being. Had he ever heard it said out loud before?

The Dagda repeated, almost chanting ritually, "This is a picture of Earth."

Giles was suddenly dizzy and the map swam before

him. Earth—the magic, mystic, forbidden word—and the Dagda said it so freely.

Above the map the globe cast a green light over the outlines of continents. Giles made an effort to focus his eyes and saw the green sphere become suddenly brighter. It began to rotate, disclosing in dimension what was flat on the picture below. The continents revolved slowly; the huge one, the tremendous land mass flanked with islands, the oceans between the other continents separated by a finger of land, swooping and tapering to points above the poles below. The white flaked poles— Giles shivered.

The Dagda's voice rang out fiercely, "Tir na nOc! Asgard! Olympus! Eden! It is all that—it is Earth!"

The women in the corner began to moan and the Dagda faced them. "Yes, weep for your homeland, for the countries of your ancestors. Mourn for it and suffer that you will never see it. Not in this picture, nor in that globe, nor in any way that man can devise. If Earth was lost before, she is truly lost now. We have turned from our beginning so completely that we now deny our origin. Weep! But remember for what you weep."

In spite of himself, in spite of everything he knew, in spite of dismay at the Dagda's emotion, Giles reacted. This mythical land—this planet that never was— attracted him. The Dagda took a long pointer and ran it over the face of the map, calling out names that rang like ghost cries in the loft.

"Asia, America, Europe—and here, the lovely islands from which our ancestors embarked—but was that their only homeland?" He paused, scanning the audience like a teacher waiting for a pupil's answer.

8

Giles looked round with mixed emotions as he saw the solemn, almost reverent way in which the group faced this man. At the end of the row in which he sat someone began to speak. He leaned forward and saw the girl. But she didn't appear reverent, only intent and serious, and her voice was low and matter of fact.

"No," she said, "the homeland was in many places, across all the seas. Asia, Africa, Europe, America—"

The Dagda nodded. "And the name of the islands from which we left?"

"Tir na nOc," the girl smiled. "Or, as it was once called, Eire, and Britain."

Britain, Eire, Africa, America—strange names. Haunting names from a mythical, imaginary past. Giles frowned, wondering why they rang with such odd familiarity. Could anyone have told him stories of the mythical Earth? More than one child in Niflhel had been corrupted by ancient fairy tales, held on the wrinkled knees of old grandmothers, rocked to sleep by feeble voices singing forbidden songs. Had he ever looked into the dim, watery eyes of his grandmother and seen shining there a dream of Earth?

Sitting amidst the hushed, attentive people, with the voice of the Dagda droning like music, Giles had a deep, swift impression of his childhood. The room and the green globe vanished and he was there again, standing outside the doorway of his hut, waving good-bye to a bent, unsteady figure. She had walked down the path of ashes to cross to her own hut a few yards away.

And then she paused, Giles remembered. She turned to look at him, a small blond boy squinting in the red glare, who had forgotten to wear his cloak and hood outside. His hair, within seconds, was covered with a layer of fine black soot. Seeing him there without cover, she removed her own hood in a defiant gesture, and held up her hands to the particles that fell on them both. She nodded her head fiercely and spoke in a stronger voice than Giles had ever heard her use before. "That's right . . . it all comes from the same source. But if we were on Earth we could be standing in the rain. You must pretend it is rain, Giles. Pretend it is rain!"

Then she walked on to her lonely hut, still bareheaded, her sparse gray hair a jet black by the time she stepped inside. And Giles stood there not minding the ash that fell on his head, fell into his eyes, parched his lips—he stood there wondering what *rain* was. And what was the difference between that rain, and this horrid black substance that curled from the ground and fell from the sky? Rain! He had no idea what it meant, but the very word made him uncomfortable and dissatisfied. He ran in to the air shower and then immersed himself in a bucket of water, using almost all of his family's supply for the week.

His parents were terribly angry when they learned, but Giles somehow knew to keep his grandmother's words a secret. The haunted word Earth he put away somewhere and tried to forget. He had—almost—forgotten until now. But the word *rain* he kept within himself and never mentioned. It was like a touchstone, a magical symbol that expressed all that might be beautiful in the invisible universe. All that was unobtainable.

It wasn't until years later that Giles learned what rain was, and that it actually did fall in Niflhel, at the poles only, during certain times of the year. And it was from this sparse supply that the entire water supply of Niflhel was drawn . . . his parents had had reason to be angry.

". . . from one of the books of Earth." The change in the Dagda's voice brought Giles back with a start, and the words that followed fell on him curiously like the word "rain" from his grandmother's lips.

". . . flowing streams, wondrous curious wells flow forth, watering the earth with pleasant streams. From the woods' middle, from the turf of Earth, each month a winsome water breaketh. . . . The groves are hung with bloom, the holy treasure of the woods wane not . . . the boughs are ever wondrous laden, the fruit new in every season. The forests fair stand green, joyously garnished . . . there is a holy perfume dwelleth in that land. . . . Never shall that know change for ever until *He* Who shaped it in the beginning shall bring His ancient Work of Wisdom unto the end."

Slowly, the Dagda closed the book and bowed his head. A strange chant followed that caused Giles to shiver—what were these words?

"An Tri numh . . ." the Dagda called.

"A chumhnadh," the audience answered.

"A chomhnadh . . ."

"A Chromraig . . ."

Then the rhythm quickened in intensity.

"An tula . . . An taighe."

"An teaglaich . . . An oidche . . . An nonchche."

"O! an oidche."

"An nochd . . . Agus gach oidche."

And the Dagda finished, "Gach aon oidche."

Giles felt extremely tense in the long silence which followed. Finally the Dagda turned away and walked into a room off the front of the loft.

Still no one moved, and Giles sat like a stone trying to

11

connect the words he had just heard with the presence of the green light that suffused the room. What was that strange language? What would it be like to live in a land where "the forests fair stand green, joyously garnished. . . ." He tried to push the thought away, to recapture his sense of the ridiculous. In a moment he would step into the streets of Niflhel and the magic of this encounter with the deviates of his world would seem like a dream.

He was hardly aware of the silent people passing by, one by one, until he realized he was alone. He rose, about to leave, when he heard a murmur of voices coming from the other room. Out of the indistinct conversation, one phrase came clear.

". . . all right. It will have to be the Branxholm, but I'm sorry to use our last retreat so soon."

Giles immediately knew he'd overheard something not meant for him. He disliked it, guessing their next meeting would be held there. He wondered if he should acknowledge his presence, but decided against it. It would only call attention to him.

He retrieved his cloak and made his way down the stairs, oddly reluctant to leave that glow of green.

When he stepped out of the doorway, the dark, gritty night of Niflhel hit him with such force he felt he had walked into a grave. He felt the shock like a physical blow and threw up his arms, as if to shield himself.

He whirled to look up again at the window. At that moment a figure cloaked in black slipped out of the shadows to stand beside him. Under a deep hood, Giles saw the intense eyes of the girl. Her face glowed pale green in the light.

12

"You don't believe in Earth, do you, Giles Chulainn?" she whispered.

How did she know his name? And what did she want him to say, Giles wondered? Again she surprised him. He wanted to speak to her, to ask why she had approached him that morning on the Underground, how she was involved in this weird cult. It was obvious that she believed in Earth . . . wasn't it? If he said yes, he might find out more about her. Giles hesitated, feeling a conflict. But something in her eyes made it impossible to lie.

"No," he answered truthfully. "No, I don't believe in Earth."

His words rolled down the empty street and echoed back to them. She listened intently, watching him, and then smiled.

"No, you truly don't believe! Good—oh, good!"

Before Giles could stop her she was gone, a dark shadowy figure lost in the dark street.

Above, the green light winked off. It was like a hope being suddenly extinguished. Giles stared after the lost, invisible globe. Good that he didn't believe in Earth? *Good?* What had she meant?

Giles would have given anything if only he could believe in the hopeless promise of that land they called "Tir na nOc"—that mythical paradise—Earth.

TWO

Giles awoke the next morning with a pounding head-ache. The gray metal walls of his hut glowed red on one side. Light from the factories came through the aperture he'd forgotten to close. There was an acrid taste in his mouth.

Slowly he came into focus, wondering why he felt so awful. A sound of air jets blowing from the shower reminded him, and he turned over, burying his head in his arms. Yes, Sigrid would be in there, removing the hours' accumulation of dust. Another day of Niflhel and Sigrid to start it for him. If he had anticipated the morning he would never have brought her home with him. But he had been unable to continue the night alone after that weird encounter with mythology.

Earth Worshippers! What had possessed him?

He groaned; his head throbbed with the aftereffects of too many drugs. He flexed his shoulders, feeling the tension and tight muscles. But he would have to get up. He pushed his legs over the side of the bed and then slowly rose, holding his head. He ran a wet towel over his face and carefully squeezed the water back through the purifier when he was finished. He dressed quickly, racing against Sigrid's entrance from the shower.

Why did he always feel such haste to say good-bye to her in the morning? Was she really so different at night? Was it just her morning gaiety that depressed him?

"Sigrid does live in the glare of day," Giles thought. "She lives in a harsh red world with things illuminated in sharp black strokes, like line drawings. And I live in another world of mosaics and strange speckles. I live in the shadows, on the other side of the sun."

No! It was nonsense, hangover thinking, a twist of words. The other side of what sun? The invisible sun of Niflhel? Giles laughed shortly at himself. He stood before the mirror combing his hair.

He hated to see his reflection, the strong face, shock of reddish blond hair, and his eyes which always looked bewildered. Every glance was a reminder that he was now eighteen—adult. He could no longer think of himself as boy or youth, he was very close to being middle-aged. It was strange how that knowledge disturbed him.

In a short time his Training period would end and he would have Senior Status in both his work and society. It was more than time for him to marry and start a family. The prospect should make him feel less lonely and bewildered, but it didn't. He still missed his own parents who had died just the year before. Perhaps he felt their loss so keenly because he was an only child, seventeen when they died at forty, as most people did— though some lived on to strange old ages, reaching even fifty and beyond.

15

"If I'm to have a child at all," he thought, "it should be now, so we could have more time together."

But the thought of bringing one more child into the world depressed him terribly. He couldn't accept Niflhel as easily as others did. He sensed a wrongness in the people, the way they grayed at twenty, died at forty. And if they did live on, as his grandmother had, in the way they aged so rapidly, became so bent and bowed and wrinkled. It was explained as "something in the air" and one day, it was said, man would discover a way of prolonging life on Niflhel. Meanwhile Giles felt something horrible in the way children were children, then adolescent, for almost half their lives, only to be propelled into becoming men and women overnight.

He felt pushed and cramped and squeezed, as if some natural promise were denied him. How would his son or daughter feel?

And who—other than Sigrid—would be the mother?

That thought depressed him even more. They had been paired for three years now and she must expect marriage. But Giles had never found, with her, that same depth of closeness and real friendship he had sensed between his mother and his father.

He desperately wanted a real friend, someone in whom he could trust completely, and confide. Suddenly he thought he saw the face of the girl from the meeting superimposed on his own, in the mirror . . . his hand with the comb stopped in mid-air.

"Oh, I must be crazy," he thought, "and immature. Still looking for fairy tales."

The sound of air jets stopped and Sigrid stepped out from the shower wrapped in Giles's long robe. She was

16

a tall, attractive girl. Long, heavy, pale blonde hair streamed over her shoulders and her cheeks glowed red from the sting of jets.

"Good morning!" she said. "You don't look well, Giles."

He kissed her and held her for a moment. "I have a headache."

"I don't wonder. You certainly took enough pleasures and forgettings." She felt his forehead. "No fever—but you really should take a remedy, Giles. I have something new and extra strong. They're in my cloak, in the inner pocket. I'll only be a little while dressing."

She smiled and pulled away slowly, going into the small dressing room, while Giles opened the closet to search within her cloak. There were enough remedies on Niflhel to keep one going through almost anything. Pills for pleasure, pain, sleeplessness, shocks, lethargy, energy, diet—and forgetfulness. A person could artificially control his entire nervous system and emotions all his life—if he wished. There were even remedies to remedy the remedies, as Sigrid had suggested. He found the new pills and swallowed two of them quickly, without water, as he'd been taught to swallow medicinal pills as a child.

His parents had never taken anything but medicine. Generally Giles didn't, either, but last night he'd taken both pleasure and forgetting without telling Sigrid what he wished to forget. He couldn't possibly have confided the strange fact of his presence at that meeting. . . .

And why didn't he feel he could confide in her? What was this vague distrust he felt—even after three years? It was really at the center of their non-marriage, and

17

perhaps it wasn't fair to her. Yet he still found himself wondering, waiting and watching—for he didn't know what—when Sigrid returned dressed and ready to leave.

They both wore the dark one-piece suits standard for working citizens. Giles helped her on with her cloak, and as his hands touched her shoulders, felt a tremor in her body. Was it this slavish physical devotion to him that he mistrusted? He knew it was there, she made that silent confession each time they were together.

"Will you have much to do today?" Sigrid asked lightly. Her tone suggested that this morning's parting was especially difficult for her. Why?

Again he saw a vision of that girl. It flashed between them like a material object, so clear that for an instant Giles thought she was actually in the room. It left him shaken.

He managed to say, "Yes, a lot to do. A whole new network of routes to be planned out to the new mines— long distances involved."

"And you'll be busy again tonight?" The suspicion in Sigrid's eyes was unmistakable. Giles shivered, wondering if she, too, had seen that vision, or sensed it. Was Sigrid that intuitive?

He lied to her gently, "Yes, I—I'm afraid I will be."

They looked at each other and the room seemed charged with unspoken thoughts. Giles longed to say something, to express himself, to be honest. But there was something like hysteria in Sigrid's eyes, almost a plea to say nothing. He wondered what would happen if they could break through this vise that held them both, in different ways, each locked in a prison of

18

unuttered words . . . and it caused him to realize something.

He felt as alone with Sigrid as he did without her.

He put on his cloak. Still in silence they left the hut to walk down the path of ash to the Underground.

It was going to be a hot day. The sun was fighting to pierce the clouds of haze that eternally obscured it. The soot sparkled in places from that effort, sending off brilliant flashes, looking like jewels scattered over the ground. It would be a day to look down, to catch as much color as possible in that reflection. The children would be out soon, shouting in glee when they saw the colors shining. They would toss it into the air, watch it fall and glitter, make huts out of the stuff, make roads and refuse mounds and Underground shafts, imitating the world in which they lived. They would be disappointed when at last their treasure of colors was gone.

It would be a bad day for mothers, whose children would be dirtier than usual. And it would be a horrible day for the Water Authority when people went slightly crazy, as they always did on such a day, and used up all their rations.

Giles and Sigrid reached the Underground entrance and stopped there to say good-bye. Although they both worked for Transportation, Sigrid would go home to work on the report she was writing, while Giles must go to the office. He was glad in some way he didn't understand that Sigrid was not continually there at Headquarters where he would have to see her each day.

"Maybe tomorrow?" he asked hesitantly and was instantly sorry. He didn't really wish to see her tomorrow.

But Sigrid smiled brightly and made it easy for him.

19

"No, I don't think so. I'm terribly busy for a while. But perhaps I'll see you at the office later." She looked almost gay as she nodded good-bye and hurried off down the path.

Either she really was busy, or had something more interesting planned, or she was an excellent actress. "She could also be covering up a sense of hurt," Giles thought guiltily. One way or the other he would have to reach a decision about Sigrid, would have to overcome this odd ambivalence.

The pills had taken full effect and Giles felt much better. All around him black-caped figures were heading for the descending elevators in the Underground shaft. He didn't wish to be squeezed in amongst them, so walked down the steps instead. A high whine in the distance told him a tube was coming and he ran down the last flight, reaching the platform just in time. The doors sealed behind him and he dropped into a seat as the tube sped out of the station. He put his head back, glad to be alone rather than in a group alcove, and closed his eyes. . . .

Instantly a picture of the green globe swam before him. Before the image faded he felt a curious sensation of warmth and relaxation, a deep inner peace that flooded his whole body. For a moment his mind was at rest and he had no thoughts. He simply luxuriated in that feeling of heat until the tube changed vibration, slowing for the next stop. Giles opened his eyes.

He was looking directly into the eyes of the girl from the meeting. But she was standing near the door, and before he could jump up or speak she turned and vanished with the crowd into the station.

20

The tube hurtled on again and the warmth left his body. A picture of those deep-green eyes remained fixed on his—and Giles felt trancelike. Had she really been here? Or was this another illusion? He felt a strange conviction that "seeing" her like this, both in his hut and here, was somehow beyond chance or accident. . . .

Who was that girl?

The question haunted him, was still with him when he left the Underground for the lower levels of Transportation Headquarters. It was the largest building in Niflhel, larger even than the Archives. After leaving his cape and showering below, he stepped onto an ascending belt that carried him in a great spiral circle around and up to his high floor.

What part of the Archives would have information on her branch of the family? If, indeed, she was descended from the Dagdas and a distant Chulainn. He wasn't even sure of that. If only he knew her first name! Family Archives were open to anyone. There'd been less than a thousand original families in Niflhel from whom everyone was descended. Tracing ancestors, finding cousins, was an acceptable pastime. Genealogy was almost a game.

He walked through a great archway to the row of office partitions, absently returning greetings from other men and women Trainees. In his own office, at the end of the building, he stood at the window looking out. Giles was training to be a Road Supervisor. One day he would be out there, leading the construction of new roads to the next group of mines. All life on Niflhel depended on the minerals and metals which were transformed, by some scientific alchemy, into clothing and

21

housing and artificial food. Below he saw the lumbering, ponderous machines leaving the city for the day's work.

Here the roads branched out like a great spoke from Headquarters. They had been here long before Giles was born, and looked old and bleak and somehow sad. He followed the straight black lines out past the city to where they disappeared in the thinnest of lines at the horizon. On beyond that flat desolate plain lay his future. New roads to link the old and new. New lines of transport to continue the deadly sameness to the next group of mines. The outlines of Niflhel had been planned generations ago.

As he did every day, Giles mentally drew a curve on one of the arrow-straight roads, twisted and turned it to break the monotony. What a relief it would be. But he had been trained to understand efficiency so thoroughly that he knew the idea was impossible. He could see and feel the increased hours of travel, the problems of building new Undergrounds. Niflhel would have to remain a block, ruled by precision lines, broken only by the high Underground shafts and the low, round buildings.

How much they owed to that ancient ancestor who had decided that at least their homes would arch and curve. Even the low mounds of huts were better than boxes. And Giles wondered in which hut that green-eyed girl lived? In which direction on one of those bleak roads?

"Room Four for Giles Chulainn. Will he please respond?" A voice from the intercom broke his thoughts.

"Right away," Giles pressed the button and answered.

It was his Supervisor with some new training problem to solve. Giles liked Master Bran Crinan, and he knew that Crinan liked him. He felt there was an unspoken agreement between them that when Giles's training period ended they would become close friends. It hadn't been possible so far because of protocol, but the time wasn't far off. . . .

As he walked to Crinan's office, Giles had a new, unheard-of thought. Could he possibly skip that waiting period and claim his teacher's friendship right now? They had worked together for three years. He trusted his teacher more than anyone he knew. Master Crinan knew of his relationship with Sigrid, if only superficially. Could he confide in him now—even tell him about that other girl? Giles wanted an excuse to leave the office and search for her in the Archives. Perhaps he wouldn't need to invent one if he told his teacher the truth.

Bran Crinan was only twenty-four but looked years older. He had a kind, craggy face that was lined and haggard looking. His hair was completely gray. He had been married for several years but still had no children, a deep disappointment to him. He was one of the unfortunate ones who aged so rapidly they could predict extra-shortened lives. Giles felt he was more serious and sensitive than anyone he knew.

He walked in with a feeling of elation and hope at the thought of leaping across that Master-Trainee relationship. But he immediately sensed something unfamiliar in the atmosphere of Crinan's office. The doors slid shut behind him and there was a thickness. . . .

Master Crinan didn't look up but nodded to a seat

beside his desk. Not meeting Giles's eyes, he said slowly, "There's never been anything in the least Contrary about you, Giles, so I'll speak freely. We've had a report that you attended a meeting of Earth Worshippers last night."

Giles was too stunned to answer.

"Perhaps you were unaware that the groups are to be Classified shortly—in a matter of days, I believe—but that's not important in your case. We're only interested in your reactions to what you heard last night. Evidently it was the first time you have ever been exposed to the Earth Worshippers. *Am I right?*"

The question came crisply and Master Crinan finally looked directly at Giles. His eyes were wide and insistent.

Giles nodded quickly. His heart was pounding with a strange new fear. He felt as if he had suddenly been transported to some utterly unfamiliar and dangerous territory. He sat very still.

"Yes," Crinan smiled, "that's what we thought."

"Who are '*we*'?" The question burst from Giles.

"The Protectors. You know we have contact with the Society here, Giles."

Yes, he knew about the Society of Protectors but he couldn't believe—"I had no idea that you—that you were involved."

"I've just become a member," Crinan said, with satisfaction, "thanks to you."

"Me—?"

"Yes. Your attendance at that meeting, just prior to Classification, Giles. You see, the Society knows we've worked together, and they'd like us to work together

24

again now, in a new way. I'm very pleased. But first
things first. As I said, they want to know your reactions
to that meeting."

Giles stared at him, lost in conflicting impressions
and questions. Who could have informed to the Society
about his presence at that meeting? Only the girl knew
his name—but, it couldn't be the girl! They must plant
their own people among the Earth Worshippers.

"Your reactions, Giles!" Master Crinan frowned.

"I—I'm not clear," said Giles. "What reactions do you
mean?"

"Well—for one thing your reaction to the idea of
Earth."

"The idea of Earth!" Giles was incredulous.

"Yes." Crinan watched him intently.

"But there's nothing to it! There is no Earth! The
whole thing's ridiculous—harmless—as far as I can see.
I don't understand why they're even bothering to Classify those groups—"

"Then you *don't* believe in Earth."

"Of course not!"

Giles resented the question. It was the same question
the girl had asked. But she couldn't have known the answer, while his teacher had worked with him, trained
him, for three years. He must know that Giles couldn't
believe in a myth.

"Good!" said Crinan.

Again it was an echo of the girl's words, and the uncanny repetition made Giles shiver.

"Then you can be of help to us." Master Crinan
smiled, leaned across the desk, and clasped his hands
together. His posture was conspiratorial, his attitude in-

25

timate. The Master-Trainee relationship had certainly vanished, but in the last way Giles would ever have expected. He couldn't believe that his teacher was engaging him in this conversation.

"It isn't going to be easy to find and abolish all those groups," said Crinan.

"Why abolish them at all?" Giles suddenly felt tired and rather sick, but he had to respond with something. "I can't see what harm they do. They're just small groups of people looking for excitement, or some belief, a fairy tale to make life easier. I should think that Classifying them would bring undue attention—"

"Ah! But that evaluation comes from attending only one meeting, Giles. And you saw everything from the outskirts of the group. From what I understand there is a real inner circle that has definite plans and objectives. And it doesn't consist of little old women sobbing over a dream."

Had Master Crinan ever attended a meeting himself, Giles wondered? How else could he know of "little old women"? He was reminded of the Dagda and those other men he had overheard speaking of using their "last retreat."

"What are their objectives?" he asked curiously.

"I'll be honest with you, Giles. We're not sure of their actual plans, so I can't offer real proof of anything. But I can tell you the Society's suspicions. We suspect they would like to revolutionize the government of Niflhel, as a preparation for making Earth the compulsory religion. Then to start out on a series of journeys—crusades, if you will—to find the planet itself."

"But it doesn't exist!" Giles cried.

"That's right," Crinan agreed, blinking into the distance. "And we hardly have the rudiments of flight, to say nothing of finding an imaginary planet—or any planet for that matter—with telescopes that can't even penetrate our atmosphere. Disregarding the fantastic idea of crusades, you can imagine our world under the domination of people committed to a dream? We'd all be living in a fool's paradise, our entire economy devoted to endless and fruitless endeavors."

"But it's out of the question," said Giles after a moment. "There could never be a revolution here. They couldn't hope to change Niflhel."

"They could," Crinan disagreed. "They'd have a very good hope if these meetings continue. The groups have been sprouting alarmingly; there's been a tremendous increase in the numbers of people attending. That's another thing we'd like to know—*why* after so many years? It's been generations since the Earth Worshippers started their cult, and until now it's been just as you said, harmless. Why is there this sudden flowering of interest?"

He surveyed Giles curiously. "Why, for example, at your age, at this particular time, did *you* go?"

The question rang true. Why *had* he gone, Giles wondered? There was the girl, of course, but wasn't there something beyond her as well? What was the mysterious mood that came over him more and more often recently? Like something not of himself but something descending upon him?

He looked at his teacher and they silently exchanged this curiosity.

"You see, it is something to consider, isn't it?" Crinan

27

said softly. "Now you must be wondering what all this has to do with you. I've been asked to become your liaison with the Society. They—and I—feel that you're stable enough to continue your contact with that group. You can bring us needed information if you agree to act as a Watcher."

"The word used to be spy," Giles said recklessly. He didn't care now if he offended Crinan, the proposal made him feel so sick inside.

"It *is* an honor," Crinan reminded him.

Giles was well aware of the extra benefits that came to members of the Society. Little things from secret sources to make life a bit easier and brighter. Did he want that? Was this sick, interior shame he felt merely an atavism? The various branches of the Chulainn family, though often active in government had never, to Giles's knowledge, entered the secret circles of the Society.

On the other hand, if everything that man had accomplished on Niflhel was to be threatened or destroyed by the mysterious growth of this Earth cult. . . .

He didn't know. He couldn't tell if this offer was really an "honor" or the first note in a descending scale.

"I can't give you an answer now, Master Crinan. I'll have to think about it."

"Good," his teacher smiled. "And if you wish to attend another meeting in the meantime, Giles, don't let this conversation stand in the way. We're quite sure of your ultimate decision."

He thrust out his hand. Giles shook it and rose to his feet, smiling mechanically.

Attend another meeting. . . .

He had liked and trusted Bran Crinan, counted on their future friendship, even looked up to him. Now he felt the full force of the man's stupidity in underestimating him. Did Crinan really expect him to swallow that statement and lead the Society directly to the next meeting place of the Earth Worshippers? It was an obvious admission they didn't know about the Branxholm!

A warm tingling began in his feet, raced up his spine and settled in the muscles of his neck, stiffening them with anger. It was a strange anger, a wish for physical violence that he had only experienced once before in his life. . . .

When he returned to his office he stared at the dark metal desk, the black walls, the streaks of soot-dotted red light that slanted through the window. He looked at the faint cloud of ash that was slowly settling at the joints between walls and floor. Not all the sealed buildings in Nifhel could keep it out; not when men, despite their cloaks and showers and precautions, brought it in continually. And not only in their hair and clothes but even, Giles realized, in their attitudes.

His own teacher, so easily enlisted in the Society, so quick to use and manipulate Giles. Why? Out of fear? Perhaps he felt he had no choice. He could also be completely sincere. He might really believe they could work together with friendship in this "new way."

No, Crinan knew better. Giles knew better. Any contact with the Society precluded truthful, open, honest encounters. The possibility of real friendship was lost, and that made Giles feel lonelier than ever.

He remained at the window looking out, still feeling

29

shocked, trying to acknowledge the fact that he was solitary, apart, truly alone in this world.

Niflhel was more than a land of metals and minerals, of rock and ash and hot smoke blowing into the obscured sky. It was a world of fearful, shrouded men, slavishly attached to the only things they knew—their short lives, round huts, blazing factories, straight roads —and always their search for the next group of mines.

"Someday those roads will encircle Niflhel," Giles thought, "and that round line will look utterly straight to our eyes. One flat, desolate plain—a web of precision around the planet dotted with huts and hooded men. Someday it will all be exactly the same. There'll be no more horizons and no more roads to build. I and others like me will have built them all."

His resistance to the vision was so strong that he was shaken. Again he felt that sweeping tide of fury. Was this all that men could do or be? Was this "achievement" what the Society so carefully "protected"?

That unknown group of men and women who maintained, and had always maintained, the continuity of life on Niflhel—who were they? Governments could come and go but the Society of Protectors and their Watchers went on forever.

He should join them immediately, according to his background, education, and training. But he couldn't deny the message in his strange new anger.

Did he have a secret wish to be Contrary himself? Giles didn't know. But he was going to do exactly what his teacher had suggested. He would go to another meeting of the Earth Worshippers—and somehow neither Bran Crinan nor the Society would ever know.

⠿⠿⠿⠿THREE⠿⠿⠿⠿

Giles had just turned fifteen on the day of his final Examination. The ritual white cloak was hanging in a sealed bag in the closet.

"Wear your black and change at school," his mother had said, taking down the immaculate cape that gleamed through the transparent bag with a strange purity.

"Oh, no!" Giles, who still felt an adolescent conformity, was horrified. "Nobody does that!"

He turned to his father. "You didn't do that, did you? We wear the black over it. I don't want to be the only one there changing in school."

His voice broke and John Chulainn smiled, both at the exaggeration and Giles's excitement. "Giles can change here, Gerta," he said. He understood very well how his son was facing the day. He remembered his own Day of Examination.

His mother saw the look that passed between them and quickly consented. "Here you are, Giles." She handed him the bag with a careful gesture that made Giles want to cry.

He swallowed hard, accepting it, accepting also the

meaning behind it. Gerta Chulainn was giving her son to his manhood. She was understandably sad, but had an obvious pride that made Giles wonder if he were truly ready.

He put on the white cloak feeling that he performed a magical rite. It was the most radiant object he had ever touched. He would wear it once only in his lifetime, on this day. And then it would be cleaned and purified again to hang sealed in a closet awaiting another generation, another Examination day. Both his father and grandfather had worn this cloak. Its whiteness symbolized the clean and permanent break between youth and manhood.

His parents watched him silently.

He drew the black cloak over that strange radiance, and went to the door. In the age-old custom of Niflhel his father gravely shook his hand and stepped back. Then his mother approached and Giles took her hand. He felt hot behind his eyes—he wanted to kiss her good-bye—but according to tradition he merely pressed her hand and left the hut.

He felt wrapped in mystery as he walked down the path. Emotions he hadn't felt before broke over him in waves. He looked toward the hut where his grandmother had lived, and died, years ago. In a gesture half real and half theatrical, he raised his hand in a parting farewell. Although he would not leave Niflhel—where else was there to go?—he felt an urge to discharge himself from all his past.

He was filled with dreams and goals and associations that tumbled wildly in his imagination. And in this young, emotional state, he walked with a proud posture toward school.

A huge clod of dirt filled with soot and small stones broke against his head. It sent him stumbling to sprawl headlong on the road. His black cloak billowed up as he fell, and his legs caught in the white cloak. It ground into the dirt as a cloud of ash arose and he choked. There was grit between his teeth. Tears sprang to his eyes—and he heard someone laugh.

Giles sprang up, creating more clouds of ash, and whirled around. Across the road another young figure in a black cape started to run. Giles darted after him with unnatural speed. In a moment he caught up and grabbed the black cape, jerking the boy back. The cape tore and the hood fell back, and Giles saw it was Car Saunders, a classmate.

They stood there looking at each other, not speaking. Saunders seemed terrified at the expression in Giles's eyes. He began to whimper. Giles felt a strange new energy rise within him. Very deliberately he smiled, and slowly took his hands away from Saunders's cloak.

The boy was paralyzed. He didn't move while Giles, still smiling, carefully removed his own black cape, and with one swift movement ripped Saunders's cape right off him. They faced each other in their white cloaks.

Giles had a picture of himself at that moment he would never forget. It was the first time he had experienced that stranger inside himself who seemed to be standing beside, looking on. He saw himself raise his arm and saw Saunders shrink back. He could have stopped right then—he saw his choice. But he also saw his shattered dream.

Saunders hadn't just thrown dirt on his graduation cloak; he had thrown all the filth of Niflhel at Giles. In that clod of dirt was the reality of the world Giles wanted to love. He would never look at Niflhel through a dream again, and for that he almost wanted to kill Car Saunders.

He lashed out with a fury that left Saunders a crumpled mass on the ground. He felt he could go on hitting him for the rest of his life. But he stopped because he knew he must. He picked Saunders up and pushed him, by the scruff of his neck, all the way to school.

Ordinarily the sight of two boys in ruined white cloaks on Examination day would have invited malicious amusement among the students. But there was something in Giles's eyes as he dragged Saunders down the corridor to the Superior's Office that stopped them from laughing. They felt only awed, and even a little frightened. Even the teachers who saw Giles that day were provoked to silence.

He kicked open the door with one foot, and entering, dropped Saunders into a chair.

Laeg Falkirk, the Superior of Giles's school, looked up from his desk. His glance traveled slowly from Giles's eyes down the ruined white cloak. Then he looked at Saunders, limp in the chair, eyes closed, breathing in short gasps.

Falkirk was an enormous, ruddy-faced man with hard eyes. He commanded instant respect from his student body and they all liked him. Parents sometimes mistrusted him. His eyes narrowed now as he stared at the boys, trying to see beyond appearances.

Giles stared back, defying him to say the wrong word, make the wrong move.

Finally Falkirk smiled. With surprising gentleness he removed Saunders and took him to the infirmary. When he returned a moment later, Giles hadn't moved. Falkirk sat down again and looked at him.

"I wonder if you wish to take the Examination now," he probed quietly.

Giles stiffened for a minute, misunderstanding. Then he saw what Falkirk meant. In a way his private ceremony for "manhood" had already taken place. And how could he appear among the rest of the white-cloaked students in that huge hall now?

"Yes," he said gratefully. "I would like to take it here with you, now."

Falkirk nodded and rose, facing Giles. "Are you ready?" he asked.

It was the first question of the official Examination.

"I am ready," Giles replied.

"Who are you?"

"I am Giles Chulainn of the Chulainns from the Dagdas, a man."

"Where are you?"

"I am on Niflhel, the planet of my birth. The planet of my ancestors' birth, of theirs before them, and of those in the beginning of time."

"Give us the history of your planet."

"In the beginning there was nothing save the sun. Then from a part of the sun was thrown a huge mass that collected itself into gasses and particles, forming the planet of Niflhel. For ages there was nothing here fit for man. Only after eons did the sparse waters come from the cold places. And of that we have seen only the beginning."

As he said this, Giles frowned, sensing something untrue. But Falkirk went on.

"Give us the history of man."

"Man had his beginning in the rock under Niflhel. Who he was then and how he looked we do not know. But there he was formed. Only after long ages did man emerge from beneath and find his place on the surface. When he came up he was fully grown, and from those early ancestors we have records."

"What are these records and where are they?"

"They are songs of praise for Niflhel. They tell of the journey from the dark caverns to the surface. They are kept in the Archives of Niflhel where all can read them."

"What of the idea that man exists on other planets in the obscured universe?"

"There is no truth in that."

"What of the idea that man could ever leave Niflhel, the planet of his birth?"

"There is no truth in that." Giles's voice became heavier, the questions more troublesome to answer.

He had learned the automatic responses as an exercise, but never before had they reached his mind and heart. Was it true? Could man never leave Niflhel? Could he, Giles Chulainn, never leave?

It was then, during the Examination, that Giles understood what he would do with his life. If there were no hope of escape, he must go as far as he could. Once a life's work was chosen on Niflhel there was no turning back; all right then, he would build roads. He would always be on the last frontier of his world. The decision, for a moment, made him feel a little better.

Falkirk continued the Examination, passing on to academic questions, and finally to the closing oath.

"Do you promise to obey the laws and customs of Niflhel? To use your manhood in aid of the development of this world?"

"I do promise that."

"Do you promise not to believe in scandalous ideas and groups which would deny our true origin?"

"I do promise that." Giles even smiled at the obvious reference to Earth Worshippers, whom no one took seriously.

"Do you promise that, to the best of your ability, you will maintain Niflhel in your inner thoughts as the best and only place for man?"

"I do promise that."

Falkirk pressed his palm against Giles's and it was over.

Giles waited to feel a change, a difference inside, now that he was a man and a citizen. But he felt nothing. Maybe one had to stand with hundreds of others in order to experience that joy and freedom people spoke of after completing Examination.

He looked down at his ripped, soot-covered cloak. Maybe one had to be cleaner.

He took off the cloak and handed it to Falkirk with an unspoken request to bury it somewhere.

"I wish you luck, Giles," said Falkirk, looking at him kindly. "If you want to keep this incident from your parents, I'll back you up. But don't forget that in many ways you had a better Examination than most."

Giles didn't understand what he meant and was suddenly too tired and depressed to ask. He wrapped himself in his black cape, pulled the hood well down around his face and quietly left the school. From the large auditorium he could hear a chorus of responses from his classmates taking the regular Examination.

Would Falkirk go now into the infirmary and give Car Saunders a private Examination, too? Giles didn't know and didn't care. He had never felt worse. He kicked at the black ground and hurried on, almost running in his haste to get away from those voices. Everything was ruined! Life was at an end when it should be beginning. Or was that just very young thinking? He had a lump in his throat and the streets of Niflhel had never looked so desolate.

It had been all right in Falkirk's office, when he was fired with righteousness and anger, but now Giles felt terribly alone and cut off. A better Examination than most!

He couldn't go home yet, his parents would know something was wrong. He couldn't spoil their day. They wouldn't be expecting him until much later, after the ceremonial banquet. Giles stopped, wondering where to go. There was an Underground entrance nearby; he could ride a long distance, perhaps to the edge of the city. He started toward it and then stopped again. He didn't wish to *ride*. On impulse, he began walking the long, long distance to the outskirts of Niflhel.

Roads! He would build them. He would always be on that last possible edge, where there was nothing between him and the horizon. He wanted to know what these roads were like, to feel them under his feet, to sense the distances. He supposed he was testing himself in some way now that he was a "man," testing his strength and his decision.

LEGEND OF LOST EARTH

He walked most of the afternoon and at dusk came to the edge of Niflhel. Here was the last elevator shaft to the Underground. He would take it home later, but first he walked on into the area beyond the city. Piles of refuse had been buried here, creating a large mound in the otherwise flat landscape. Giles liked the sight of that rising ground.

He climbed up, and going down the other side saw another black-caped figure sitting at the bottom, staring off into the distance. Warily, Giles approached. He couldn't turn back now, he'd been seen. It was a girl, he realized with surprise.

"What are you doing here?" Giles blurted out. It was incredible to find a girl sitting at the city dump, looking out at nothing.

"What are you doing here?" she repeated promptly.

Something in her voice gave him an odd reaction. It was a nice voice, but had a strange timbre. He walked closer, curious to see what she looked like.

"Hello, Giles," she said.

He sat down beside her, frowning. It was a girl named Sigrid whom he knew slightly—they lived in the same area—but why hadn't he recognized the voice?

"Hello," he said. "I'm sorry I didn't recognize you. You look—seem—different."

"I know," she said. "I am different."

Giles heard it now, an unfamiliar, husky tone. "The girls' Examination wasn't today, was it?" he asked.

"No, not yet," she looked at him and smiled. Then she leaned back on the mound of dirt, putting her arms under her head.

39

"What are you doing here?" he repeated.

"You wouldn't believe me if I told you, so I won't tell you."

He suddenly realized she was very pretty. "Yes, I would. I'd believe you."

"Well, I'm doing what you're doing. I'm looking at Niflhel."

"No, you're not," he said sadly. The shock of her presence had gone, and he felt the day coming back to him. "You're looking out beyond Niflhel."

"Still, the important thing is that I'm doing just what you're doing." She turned over on one elbow and looked up at him. "I wish you'd tell me what happened today. I saw you dragging Car Saunders through the street."

"You weren't supposed to be out!" Giles gasped. Examination Day for both boys and girls was a rigidly separated, private affair.

"I wasn't out. I was looking through a window. I wanted to see you on your way to the ceremony."

"But why?" he asked, puzzled. "I mean, we're not related, you're not a cousin or anything. I don't even know you that well."

"Not yet," Sigrid smiled again and fastened her eyes on his. He couldn't look away. She shook the hood off her head and a mass of heavy blonde hair came cascading down her shoulders. Giles wanted terribly to touch it.

"You'll get dirty," he warned, looking at her hair.

"It doesn't matter. Tell me about Saunders."

"I don't think I can," Giles started. "It wasn't much anyway. He just threw something at me." The sight of the hair was too much, and tentatively he put out a hand.

"Go on, what else?" Sigrid urged.

"Well, there was a fight—" Giles stopped as his hand touched the amazing softness of her hair. It startled him. He had never touched a girl before, and he suddenly didn't know if he wanted to bury his face in that honey-colored mass, or if he wanted to take it violently and pull it.

The shock of that conflict, on top of so many other conflicting emotions, loosened his timidity. He grabbed Sigrid by the shoulders and stared down at her. *"What are you doing here?"* he whispered fiercely, remembering that he had come here to be alone, to look, to think—

Instead of answering she put her arms around him and drew his face down to hers. There was something wonderful and terrible about it. Giles felt he was descending to the heart of Niflhel. He wanted to resist and emotionally he tried to—emotionally he was somewhere else. But the force of her wish captured him physically and within minutes he knew nothing more than the instinct of his own body drawing him even deeper in a descent to Sigrid and Niflhel.

At fifteen, on Examination Day, Giles may have learned more than any other boy in the city. He had found his strength, decided his future, learned what it was to be alone, and with Sigrid had discovered himself as a man.

He also learned, though he was too young then to admit it, that neither his strength, nor work, nor Sigrid, nor Niflhel—especially Niflhel—would ever be enough for him.

⠿⠿⠿ FOUR ⠿⠿⠿

It was that day of Examination that Giles remembered when he left Headquarters in the late afternoon. The first person who had evoked real violence in him was his classmate, Car Saunders. And now his teacher, Master Crinan. Giles felt it wasn't so much the man himself, however, as his own deep disappointment, shock, and sense of loss.

Who in Niflhel could really be trusted?

He had no doubt that Crinan was his Watcher, regardless of words about "liaison" and "working together." Giles knew how the Society worked. Everyone did while pretending they didn't. Crinan was watching him, someone else was watching Crinan, and there was probably a third party watching them both.

He hadn't dared leave the building today to search for that girl in the Archives. And now if he wished to reach the Branxholm without being detected, he would have to take a circuitous route.

He decided, when he entered the Underground tube, to change two stations later and circle back. Meanwhile, his thoughts remained fixed on questions of trust, and Examination Day, and Sigrid. It had been more than a year later before she finally confessed to having followed him that day to the city's edge. She had waited for him after school, seen him walking, and guessed his direction. She had gone before him on the Underground and deliberately waited for him at the refuse dump. Each time Giles remembered that day and her confession a year later he re-experienced the same helpless fury. It was like a betrayal of something deep and serious within him. And now he wondered if that intentional act of hers, three years ago, was the basic flaw in their relationship? Would it be different now if he had been the one to seek her out? And at a different time.

He'd been on a different level that Day of Examination, and within all his confusion and hurt, had been seeking something. What might he have found if he had not found Sigrid? What questions might have been answered? His search had been turned that day in a way he hadn't intended and Laeg Falkirk couldn't have dreamed. Sigrid and Saunders. They had both acted on him. One breaking his dreams of Niflhel, the other creating another dream—really putting another Niflhel in the place of the one he had lost.

Yet that other world, with Sigrid, had carried him through, hadn't it? How would these years have been without their relationship and everything connected with it? Without that one human contact and superficial search for pleasure most citizens pursued all of their lives?

The tube whined to a stop at the first station and Giles thought again of the girl's face this morning when he had felt that curious warmth. What was this deep difference he sensed between them? He felt it organically, throughout his whole body, even though he knew

43

nothing about her. Perhaps, Giles thought, if it hadn't been for Sigrid, he might have found her.

He might even, he smiled whimsically, have found Earth! Or the dream of Earth.

Again he wondered at his actions last night, in going to that meeting, and what was he doing now on this fantastic trip to the Branxholm?

Giles hurried off the tube at the next stop and circled back to Headquarters. There he descended an elevator for another tube leading to the far periphery of Niflhel. He watched the other passengers closely and couldn't tell whether anyone was observing him or not. But he'd better not chance it. Instead of going to the end of the line, he abruptly exited at the stop before, and took an elevator up. So far he was alone.

The streets above were deserted and the night was even worse than the last. He pulled down his visor to shield his face from the dust that was blowing like a small storm and quickly cut through an arcade leading between two streets. He slipped into a doorway and waited for a long time, listening for any sound, watching for any hint of a shadow. There was nothing.

Finally convinced he wasn't being followed, Giles began walking freely to the edge of the city.

In an odd way he felt he was repeating the journey of his fifteenth year. He had come full circle, but something within him had changed, and another search was beginning. What this search was for he couldn't have explained to anyone, not even himself. It felt like a small, centered, bright core, that was separated from feelings of disappointment, betrayal, hurt, and loss. It was, on the inside, a little like seeing that green globe from the outside—a tiny flame of hope.

And it was just as vague. Giles knew only one thing. This time, he would remain alone and protect that core of hope. This time no one would invade and spoil his search . . . whatever it was for.

At the outskirts of the city, Giles paused, aware that his heart was beating rapidly. He was strangely excited. Was it just this solitary journey on this filthy night? Or that for the first time in his life he was being Contrary and going against all the rules of Niflhel?

He looked up, sensing a new mystery about the obscured sky. There *was* a sun, though it was never seen. Could there be another sun somewhere—and another planet? A green, life-giving planet different from Niflhel? There was even something wrong with the *name* of his home, thought Giles. One name for the planet and the one city on it. He gazed at the dark horizon, streaked with red and black, until a cloud of brown dust swept across and blocked his view.

It was the girl! *She* was the cause of his sense of mystery and excitement. Not wild thoughts of the universe or even wilder wishes for a different home. Perhaps *she* was the cause of his search—that core of hope —and his wish for an end to loneliness.

The Branxholm was still a long distance off. As Giles plodded on through the dirt, following the half-buried tracks that had once led there, he wondered why the Earth Worshippers would choose it as a meeting place. It seemed too obvious.

Years ago a group of profit-seeking men had built the huge, round dome as a cathedral to pleasure. A wagon, called the Gondola, had sped along these tracks to that last, lonely building on the outskirts of Niflhel. Then it was possible to sit in the Branxholm and gaze at the

45

horizon while eating the most exotic foods that the Master Chefs could invent from their limited, artificial resources. One could watch, at the same time, the very best entertainment the city had to offer. But the new factories had spoiled all that. Geysers of smoke billowed up now to cast a pall across the horizon. There was no distance to be viewed except for a few moments at a time. The Branxholm was a deserted place, a ruin that would soon crumble away if it were not torn down to make way for new roads.

Giles approached that dark, lonely outpost beyond Niflhel. It rose like a ghostly half-circle from the ground. Once he had been here with Sigrid, and then it had been brilliantly illuminated. Now only lingering red light from the factories reflected from one side. There was no light from within. No dim green light shining as a beacon. He was oddly disappointed, even though he knew they couldn't announce their presence with a globe.

He made his way to the entrance with difficulty. Soot had piled up waist high against the huge double doors. He sank deeply into the dirt as he pushed against them. Nothing happened. Angrily, Giles pushed again. This journey mustn't end with nothing. He couldn't have been mistaken in what he'd heard at the meeting. . . .

Dirt rose under his cape and settled in his clothes and shoes. He sank deeper in it as he pounded on the doors. Was there a signal that he didn't know? A secret knock —or another entrance?

He heard a very faint sound from behind. Before he could even turn his head to look he felt the thrust of a sharp needle through his cape and into his arm. . . .

Giles blacked out instantly.

He felt warm, much too warm, and instinctively thrashed off the cloak that covered him. His eyes opened slowly on a world of shifting green haze. He tried to lift his head but the slight motion made him ill and dizzy. He sank back again, eyes closed, hearing only faintly the sound of many voices chanting together.

When he awoke again, Giles's eyes focused with more clarity, but still the images seemed to float before him. He perceived a figure clothed in green. Sounds of a melodious voice, half chanting, half singing, drifted toward him.

> *I am the wind which breathes upon the sea,*
> *I am the wave of the ocean,*
> *I am the murmur of the billow . . .*

Straining to see more clearly, Giles lifted himself on one arm. He was lying on a pile of rugs in a huge chamber lighted by many green lamps along the walls. The texture of the enclosure was rough, unlike any building he knew, more like a mine excavation. He looked up dizzily and could not find the ceiling. The walls seemed to rise without end. . . .

He peered back, squinting, to the figure chanting in the distance. He thought it was the girl, standing in back of a fire, while grouped around it, sitting in a large circle, were a number of people listening quietly.

> *I am the ox of the seven combats*
> *I am the vulture upon the rocks*
> *I am a beam of the sun . . .*

Her arms were uplifted and her head was thrown high—Giles felt that she was standing out of doors—

that she was standing in a clear sun. Then she dropped
her head and her eyes traveled the length of the chamber. She seemed to be looking directly at him.

> *I am the fairest of plants,*
> *I am a wild boar in valor*
> *I am a salmon in the water*
> *I am a lake in the plain . . .*

The words sank into Giles as if they had material
substance, and he thought the girl seemed to change
shape as she stood there behind the fire. What did these
odd words mean?

> *I am a ward of science*
> *I am the point of the lance of battle*
> *I am the God who creates in the head of man the*
> *fire . . .*

Then her voice changed tone. She rose, standing on
tiptoe and threw up her arms in challenge, the words
ringing out like wild bells:

> *Who is it who throws light into the meeting on the*
> *mountain*
> *If not I?*
> *Who announces the ages of the moon*
> *If not I?*
> *Who teaches the place where couches the Sun . . .*
> *if not I?*

Giles felt a deep shudder, a trembling rush through
him, and then the girl darted away from the fire and
was gone. He lay back, exhausted, as another chant
began in that unknown language. It drifted past him.

He was filled with the words, "Who teaches the place where couches the Sun. . . ?"

He closed his eyes and felt the touch of a hand on his forehead before he fell deeply asleep once more.

When he woke at last his head was completely clear. The chamber, or cavern, was empty and the fire was gone. The Dagda was sitting beside him, and as Giles sat up on the pile of rugs, handed him a cup of water.

Giles drank it slowly. Seeing the older man so closely now he was struck by the sense of purpose that seemed to lie behind his eyes. He must be over sixty, an incredible age for Niflhel, and yet he had an air of dedication and vigor.

"You're a Chulainn," the Dagda stated when Giles handed back the cup. His blue eyes probed deeply, and Giles nodded.

"Then we are cousins. Many of our family have come to refresh their memories of Earth. I noticed you last night. It was your first time with us, wasn't it?"

"Yes, my first time."

"And you found it interesting?" His eyes never left Giles's, who felt he was being evaluated in some way. It was uncomfortable, disquieting.

"Interesting, yes—" In spite of his innate respect for this man, Giles felt some irritation. He had some questions to ask himself. And where was the girl? She had vanished, and he had really come seeking her. "Interesting and untrue, of course."

"Then you didn't find that your racial memories of Earth were evoked?"

"How could there be racial memories of something

49

that doesn't exist?" Giles returned shortly. "You might ask me about my racial memories of Niflhel!"

The Dagda was silent and Giles regretted his tone. It disturbed him, though, that one of his own family would be involved in something as dreamlike and useless as this Earth cult. Particularly this old man whom he instinctively liked.

"You know," he said more gently, "I really think there's something dangerous about these groups. You're only creating illusions and fantasies for people, wishes that can never be fulfilled."

He waited for a response but the Dagda simply watched him. Giles thought of what Crinan had said about an inner circle with the aim of revolution. He knew it was ridiculous. He struggled on, trying to express his thoughts.

"Look, it might be different if you regarded Earth as it is—a fairy tale, a myth. If the groups were just for entertainment. But you've been creating an actual religion around this old legend! I think that endangers the well-being of Niflhel. And now your own groups are in danger, as you said yourself last night."

The Dagda didn't reply to anything Giles had said. He asked only, "So you do not believe in Earth?"

Wasn't it obvious? Giles frowned—why did the man even ask? "Of course not!"

"He is the one I told you of." The girl was suddenly beside the Dagda. She had come from the shadows behind them, and stood with one hand resting on the old man's shoulder. Instead of the green gown she now wore a long white robe. She looked down at Giles and smiled.

"My niece, Lir Regan." The Dagda introduced her

absently. He rose, as if coming to a decision. "Come along, then, Giles Chulainn, if you are the one."

So they were distantly related, Giles thought as he stood up, staring at her. Lir Regan—an odd name—one he hadn't heard before. She smiled back at him quietly until the Dagda began to walk away and then turned to go with him.

Giles would have followed her anywhere. But a certain stubborn pride made him linger. "First I'd like to know why I was drugged from behind. I'd like to know where I am!" he called after the Dagda.

The old man turned. "Have we asked you yet how you knew of the Branxholm? Have we accused you of being a Watcher?"

Giles stared at him.

"There are many questions to be answered, but my niece is seldom wrong. Therefore you are first going to hear the true history of Niflhel."

He walked off and Lir Regan followed. Giles hesitated only for a moment and then fell in behind them. The lights along the walls cast green shadows before them. They walked silently. Giles looked down and saw that slippers had been placed on his feet, and that he was strangely free of soot. Then he realized what was singular about this place—wherever it was—it was pure and clean. There wasn't a particle of soot underfoot, not a speck blowing anywhere. He looked up and still couldn't find the ceiling of the huge cavern. But they must be deep underground, he thought, and was sure of it when the Dagda led him through an archway into a long tunnel. It led down, and here the ceiling was low, the stone had not been worked. The sides were rough and jagged.

51

He walked faster to catch up with the Dagda and Lir Regan. "Where *are* we?" he called, his voice echoing in the tunnel. "Is the Branxholm above us?"

"Shh!" Lir Regan answered. "It doesn't matter. You know we are beneath Niflhel."

She was smaller than Giles had remembered, much shorter than he. Her long black hair framed her face and her green eyes regarded him cautiously. Giles knew she would say no more right now.

The people he had seen before were absent. There wasn't a sign of human presence. The Dagda stopped beside a low opening in the side of the tunnel, and bending down, entered. Here there was no light, only a deep blackness. Giles couldn't walk upright, he had to crouch, and he couldn't see ahead. Lir Regan reached back for his hand and led him on several feet, then she whispered, "Now lie down flat, you'll have to crawl. Just follow me."

Feeling cold rock beneath him, and sensing the girl moving ahead, Giles began to crawl. Rock pressed down from above and along the sides. They were in such a narrow tunnel that Giles had difficulty breathing. He began to feel suffocated, and with it came a terror of enclosed places. The space grew even smaller and he sensed the enormous weight pressing on him from above. He could no longer hear the breathing of Lir Regan or the Dagda, and wondered if he had taken a wrong turn. He panicked and pushed through the tunnel harshly. A jagged rock cut deeply into his shoulder —and then suddenly he was free.

He crawled out into an open space and lay flat taking deep breaths. Then he was aware of light. Looking up he saw they were in a lofty, circular cave, illuminated by a cluster of green lights hanging far above.

Slowly, Giles rose to his feet, his heart pounding as he took in a world he'd never seen before. Hanging all the immense distance, from the roof of the cave to the floor, were enormous pictures. . . .

No—they were cloth of some kind. Not the synthetic material Giles was accustomed to. They were hangings, richly colored, with the most fantastic scenes.

Trancelike, Giles walked closer and saw the material was not smooth, but woven somehow, into those splashes of color. He stepped back to see the scale.

One of the hangings was a woodland scene. There were the "forests fair" and the "winsome water," a curl of wetness winding between the trees.

Trees! Giles had never seen a tree. How did he know?

Grouped in graceful postures beneath the sun-dappled leaves were people; naked children laughing, adults talking to each other—and other strange, four-legged creatures lying on the ground—the green, green ground.

What were they? They looked alive, but there was no life besides man. . . .

Lir Regan touched his arm, and Giles looked down to see that he was bleeding. It made no impression on him. He heard Lir Regan tear a piece off her robe and rip it into strips. He was hardly aware of the bandage being wound around his shoulder. He had eyes only for another hanging that took his breath away.

It was a high, jagged mountain, rising from the ground almost to the sun, it seemed to Giles. A spired peak, covered with snow. The pinnacle soared to the clouds and burst through above. While below the ground was not flat—it rose and fell and broke in different formations, each different and unique, nothing the same. . . .

Lir Regan tightened the bandage and touched his hand, saying, "Come." She led him to the other side of the cave where there were stacks of shelves reaching to the ceiling. Row after row of books, ancient books bound in some unfamiliar material.

Giles put out his hand to touch one, and drew it back in shock. The covering seemed alive in some way. He moved away nervously, and found the Dagda looking at him with a soft smile.

Giles shivered violently. The cave was like ice. The Dagda was wrapped now in a long, heavy cloak. Lir Regan took another from a stack on the floor and handed it to Giles. The Dagda threw some more robes on the cold rock floor and motioned Giles to sit down. Lir Regan was already seated, her eyes misty and far away as she looked at the hangings.

The Dagda took one of the books and sat facing Giles. "I said that you would hear the true history of Niflhel. But in order to understand it, it is first necessary to hear the history of Earth." He opened the book on his lap.

The words, reverberating in the cave, fell on Giles like a shower of thunderbolts. He listened, trembling under the impact.

*In the beginning God created the heaven
and the earth.
And the earth was without form, and void,
and darkness was upon the face of the deep. . . .*

54

᠁᠁᠁FiVE᠁᠁᠁

Giles awoke to feel the synthetic material of his own
bed coverings. His half-opened eyes fell upon the familiar gray metal walls of his hut. How long had he
been here? It seemed as if an eternity had passed. He
had no recollection of anything beyond the Dagda's
voice. Had he crawled back through that suffocating
tunnel? Had they brought him home? Or was it all
nothing but a dream?

He tried to sit up but his head was still swimming,
either from another drug or perhaps the influence of
those frightening words. . . . Words that didn't seem
to come from the Dagda, but from some other infinitely
remote and ancient place.

And he remembered the Dagda's own words when
he had started to explain. Giles's eyes closed and he saw
strange pictures against the darkness, forming and dis-
solving and flowing in a vast panorama. That group of
scientists—what had the Dagda called them? They
were oddly named after the different countries and continents across the seas of Earth. . . .

Earth! Giles turned in his bed, trying to dismiss the
picture of a marbled blue-and-white globe hanging in

space. He tried not to see immense reaches of blue water and green land—but he couldn't block out the images.

He saw that group of men and women gathering together in a desperate attempt to avert the catastrophe that threatened their world. What that danger was, Giles couldn't see nor understand clearly—there were only images of towering clouds and pillars of flame rising from all the cities of Earth. And after the flames, that group of scientists racing against time to save some small portion of humanity.

The story the Dagda told took on dimension, and Giles lay back exhausted, allowing the pictures to unfold.

They had come from far-flung corners of the world to one small island, so strangely named, Britain. Everywhere across the Earth, city had met city in a wild explosion of population and industrial growth. The fair green hills and valleys sagged under the weight of civilization, rotted under metal and concrete. Across whole continents the disease of industry spread while the life-giving air and the seas and oceans of Earth were dying. Almost all of Earth was dying, gutted, plundered, while heads of state still snapped at each other in bitter economic argument.

But had it been man's doing in the end? Had man destroyed himself, or had nature at last rebelled? The Dagda's words had evoked a picture of forces, first light as mist, then dark and pervasive as heavy fog, that had steamed from the hidden land, choking and changing the minds and hearts and spirit of men; that blinded men in positions of power and created rage in the emotions of the people.

56

When disaster struck, that group of scientists, hidden deep in the rock of that one island, hadn't seen the sky that suddenly flared red across the world—but they knew. Too late to avert the end, they sought another way to save themselves and those who sheltered with them. Beyond that deadly sky there were other suns, other planets . . . man had ventured into space before . . . could they now escape and save this small nucleus and seed of mankind?

There the images began to fade. Giles saw only dimly and very far away a long procession of men and women and children. He saw a spinning, something like a pale sun streaking away—but where? Beyond the earth, beyond the sun, beyond the distant stars?

He moaned and tossed feverishly. None of it was true. It was myth, it was legend, he had dreamed it. There was only Niflhel, only the flat, ash-strewn rock of this barren planet. This Niflhel, land of his birth, land of his ancestors. The Dagda was insane. He and other dreamers like him had invented this land called Earth.

But could the Dagda have invented those words?

Giles sat up and stared blindly while the memory of them echoed. No, the Dagda could not have invented those words, nor could any man born of Niflhel.

. . . and there went up a mist from the Earth and watered the whole face of the ground. . . .

He turned over, and burying his head in his arms, felt for the first time since childhood, his own tears.

Master Crinan was angry. There was no mistaking his attitude as he coldly surveyed Giles.

"Where were you yesterday and the night before?"

57

It was something his teacher had a right to know. How could he answer for a day of absence? What lie could he invent for the Society? And where had he been? Giles was exhausted.

"I don't know, Master Crinan, I was ill and that's all I know."

It was the truth. He thought he had spent yesterday lying in bed. He remembered being terribly hot. A fever? Something. He was rarely ill, but yesterday had come and gone like a nightmare. He didn't think he'd eaten anything, or even slept. He remembered only his visions and those but vaguely.

Crinan wasn't unaware of Giles's appearance. Some of the anger left him and he said more kindly, "I believe you, Giles. It's all right. However, the Society—"

"I accept!" Giles said quickly, anticipating him. "They want an answer, don't they? The answer is yes. I will join you, I will act as Watcher."

"Very good, Giles!" Crinan smiled. "You made the right decision, but I was sure you would. Now, I want you to go home and take another day off." He put a hand on Giles's shoulder and ushered him to the door. "I can see you're still not well. Later on I may have orders for us and we could be quite busy. I need you fully rested."

Giles left Headquarters grateful for Crinan's suggestion. He knew it could as easily be a direct "order" from the Society as a concerned thought from his teacher. They must be suspicious of his absence, and if he had really lost a "follower" the other night, they probably suspected he had gone to another meeting. Possibly they didn't care—as long as he agreed to join them.

They might think anything—that he was in reality a secret Earth Worshipper himself—or not—or that he had been briefly tempted and become convinced of the folly of the groups. It didn't matter what they thought. At least the affair was settled and they would never guess his real reason which lay between these extremes.

As an official Watcher he would be in a position to help Lir Regan and her uncle when Classification came. In assuming his responsibility, however, Giles knew he might also be accepting the role of protector for the entire group. If he sensed anything about Lir Regan and the Dagda, it was certain they wouldn't accept personal protection at the expense of others.

Lir Regan—even her name haunted him, gave him an ache inside. Let her sing and chant and fill herself with dreams and myths of an imaginary Earth. That didn't matter, either. She was there, and real, and Giles felt as if she held all the promise of life and love and friendship so far denied him. . . .

How strange! How absurd it was! Because of one girl he'd been near only twice in his life, and one old man whom he hardly knew, he was about to play the most dangerous double-game possible. He might also have to mingle with a group of misty-eyed people whose beliefs he didn't share and about whom, actually, he cared very little.

He rode home dead tired, not even caring to look and see whether anyone was following him or not.

At midnight he heard an insistent, ongoing buzz at the door. Finally rising to answer it, Giles realized he had slept all day and into the night. His body moved freely and he felt rested and alert. He was surprised to find Sigrid at the door, flushed and excited. She had a key.

"Why didn't you just come in?"

"It's official business, Giles," she said. "We have to be careful. I told Crinan I was coming here to get you. Please hurry and get dressed now—it's started."

He slowly closed the door, a lick of fear moving inside him. "What has started?"

"Classification! The law has just been passed. Earth Worshippers are illegal now—fully Contrary. We're picking them up and you're needed for identification. Oh, Giles!" She impulsively embraced him, "I'm so glad you accepted!"

He held her automatically, trying to subdue a sudden trembling and then looked into her eyes. "You're also a Watcher?"

Giles knew the answer before she nodded.

"Yes, of course I am, I always have been." Sigrid shook back her hood and the mass of long golden hair tumbled over her black cape. She smiled up at him. "But we can talk about it later. Please hurry—"

"Just a moment." He held her. "*Always* a Watcher, Sigrid?" he questioned softly. "Not three years ago—"

"On your Examination Day? Of course. I'd joined the Society before then."

"You were with them even on that day," he said.

"I wanted so much to tell you, to bring you in with us. But I—well, they thought it best to wait."

"For what?" he asked tightly. "Wait for what?"

"For you to be completely convinced that you didn't believe in Earth. We all expected you to go to a meeting much sooner, Giles—"

"*Why? Who* expected?"

60

"Don't be angry—" She pulled away with a puzzled frown. "You must know the Society is extremely cautious. Your grandmother had leanings in that direction. And your mother and father—we investigate."

"They were never Contrary!" Giles said furiously.

"I know, but they were considered dubious citizens. I'm sorry, Giles, but it's true. Even Laeg Falkirk, the Head of your school—"

"Falkirk!" Giles seized on the name. It made him sick to hear Sigrid speak of a secret investigation of his parents and his grandmother—but Falkirk? Falkirk who had been so kind that day, who had told Giles he had "a better Examination than most." Was that why? Falkirk, an Earth Worshipper?

"He was picked up ages ago," Sigrid said casually. "I was absolutely sure that you could never believe in such a myth. But you see, Giles, you were surrounded by these uncertain people. So you had to go to a meeting first—before we could approach you. We were waiting for the right moment. I've been waiting three years!"

"So it was you who had me followed to that meeting and informed to the Society," said Giles, feeling cold.

"And I suggested Crinan for your liaison. I know you've enjoyed working with him—but there's no time now, Giles. Please get ready. You must come to identify people."

"Classification has never meant picking people up and detaining them, has it?"

"Until now," Sigrid corrected. "But now we have to find and hold them, they must be questioned. These groups will have to stop—"

"What happened to Laeg Falkirk?" Giles asked abruptly.

"I don't know, Giles." She looked away vaguely. "I never heard of him after that one time. I was only interested in *you*. And you have nothing to worry about now, believe me." She put a hand on his arm and smiled. "You're under my direction."

He was unable to smile back. He turned away, trying to subdue that same helpless fury he had felt before, when she had confessed to following him on Examination Day. But this new betrayal was worse than he could ever have imagined. Three years of dishonesty! Three years based on a lie. What had their relationship been? Perhaps Sigrid was fond of him, had at least wanted him sexually, but she had originally wanted him for the Society. And now, after three years of pairing, he was under her "direction."

That meant she was Bran Crinan's superior, too—was responsible for enlisting him. How far up in the Society was she? He had thought he knew this girl intimately, had recently felt confused, sorry, and guilty about his emotions toward her, and his new feeling about Lir Regan. He had even felt pity, mixed with that odd distrust. Now, Giles knew that distrust was the wrong label. It wasn't distrust he felt toward Sigrid—it was fear. And he had been right to fear what awaited them outside.

The thick walls of the hut had muffled the sound, but as they stepped out they were assaulted by wave upon wave of high screeching sirens. The sky was a glaring network of sweeping, criss-crossing searchlights, probing the streets. The vibrations from the sirens had picked up all the loose dirt from the ground and spun it savagely into the air. They walked into an inferno of yellow light streaked with red and dotted with the erratic mosaic of black soot.

At the corner of Giles's street a barricade had been erected and in front of it a group of hooded Watchers were examining a long line of people. It didn't seem as if they'd found a real cell of Worshippers; they seemed to be indiscriminately questioning all the residents of the area.

"Do you recognize any of them?" Sigrid asked over the whine of the sirens.

Giles heard a new tone in her voice, an elation that was almost brutal. He looked anxiously at each face as they moved down the barricade, hoping to show no sign if indeed he did recognize anyone from the meetings. Sigrid watched him intently.

The people stood quietly, apparently unaffected by this sudden and unprecedented examination. Giles looked for a sign of anger or resistance to this intrusion into their lives. Instead he was dismayed to see only a sheeplike surrender to authority. He knew many of them by sight, but he was glad to see there was no one from either meeting of the Earth Worshippers.

As he relaxed with the relief of that, he saw the scene suddenly as if it were a moment of madness. The sirens screamed in his ears until he was one with the vibration. In Sigrid's eyes there was insanity. In the stiff postures of the guards moving the people along with mechanical precision there was insanity. The movement of Watchers racing up the street was a dance of madness that merged with the soot and the searchlights. The mounds of dwellings looked to Giles like graves housing dead people who had been resurrected to play their parts in a macabre imitation of life.

What are we dead to? Giles wanted to scream. At

that moment the sirens stopped and the people caught in that sudden vacuum of sound stopped, too, their bodies still carrying the echo.

Giles had to get away. He felt if he stayed one more moment he too would become lost in this current of insanity. He thought of the caves beneath the Branxholm with a clean, clear feeling, as if there he could become whole again, or at least find what small part of him was not already corrupted with the filth of Niflhel.

He turned to Sigrid, his mind leaping with inventions, and saw that her attention had shifted to the group of Watchers before the barricade. "You may let these people go," she said.

Giles realized she had understood, just by watching him, that there was no one worth detaining. It was frightening. He filed away this new knowledge of Sigrid's quick perception as something he would have to remember, and take into account.

"You'd better come along to the next block with me." Sigrid took his arm under the cape and led him past the Watchers. Her body was tense and determined. Giles felt his best chance was to correspond to her mood with a physical invention—a quick action that wouldn't leave room for thought.

He pressed her arm as they walked along, looking at her with a smile. Then he glanced over his shoulder at the barricade they had just left, narrowing his eyes.

"Wait a minute!" He held her when she stopped in surprise. "There is someone from the meeting there, I think." He stood rigidly, peering back at the people who were slowly dispersing and returning to their huts. Sigrid made a motion of impatience.

"No—" He held tighter, pretending to recognize

someone. "I'm sure of it!" Releasing her with a quick movement, he broke away before she had a chance to follow.

She stood watching after him as he ran down the road yelling, "That one!" and beckoned the Watchers to follow. The activity, coming in the middle of the silence, created confusion at the barricade. People who had been in line broke hastily away to let the Watchers run past. Giles, leading them on, ran wildly up one street and down another, shouting directions as he went until all the Watchers were apart, covering different streets.

He ran on, apparently in determined pursuit, until he had left them all behind and was well away from his own residential area. Then he stopped, panting for breath. The wail of the sirens began again, either for his nonexistent victim, or for another detention in a different part of the city. It didn't matter. The noise was an effective aid to his own movements.

He had carried it off! If Sigrid didn't suspect—and he hoped the swiftness of his action had been sufficient to throw her off guard. Whether she suspected or not, however, he must reach his next objective. He was so sickened by what he had learned, and seen, and understood tonight, that he didn't want to think about Sigrid.

The Watchers could have already flushed out that last secret meeting place at the Branxholm—or Lir Regan and the Dagda could still be hiding there. If he could find them in time to give warning. . . .

Behind him the sirens screamed even higher. Giles shut out the sound and walked along as if nothing existed but the cold, soot-free air of the caves, and the white gown and clear eyes of Lir Regan.

SIX

He found the cave again. Or rather his body found it for him. His senses seemed to have an intelligence of their own. The large front doors had been open this time, and he had entered the Branxholm immediately knowing the direction of a passageway down. He found the rough-hewn steps leading to the lower levels and the large chamber of the meeting. He traced his way back through the labyrinth of tunnels and crawled back to this cold high cavern with the preposterous hangings. There was no sign of Lir Regan or the Dagda —or the Watchers. The Branxholm was deserted.

Giles sat wrapped in a heavy robe gazing at the hanging with the peak of white that met the sky. His eyes traveled from the mountain to the scene of water and trees.

The cave was so silent he heard a ringing in his ears. Beyond, he caught an echo of Lir Regan's words. . . .

Who throws light into the meeting
on the mountain. . . .
Who teaches the place
where couches the sun. . . ?

Sun! What was the sun of Niflhel? A hot red globe obscured by heavy clouds. He looked at the sunlight woven into the hanging, dappling the ground beneath the trees. He would rather think of that sun supporting a clean and radiant land. Was it possible that he was beginning to believe in Earth? No, but he might have reached the point so many reached, who turned to the worship of that imaginary land. He was beginning to understand it.

To remain in Niflhel required blindness. If one saw even a little more—as he had seen the insanity tonight —Niflhel became impossible. One had to turn to something else, and where was there to turn, if not to Earth— the dream of Earth? It was better than this reality.

Yet this was his home, the land which had given him birth. A man should love his origin, should wish to cherish and improve it. He should accept this reality and not wish for another. . . .

Should. Perhaps the word was no longer in his vocabulary. Tonight he had seen the inner workings of Niflhel as he had never known them to be before. The Society of the Protectors—what was their true function? He couldn't think of it, couldn't think of all he had learned from Sigrid, and seen in her. It was too horrible, too different from what he'd always believed. . . .

Giles jumped up. He had been dreaming here too long, hoping that Lir Regan and her uncle might appear. It must be nearly dawn by now. He could crawl back through that tunnel and search for them elsewhere. There might be even deeper passages and caverns where the groups were hidden.

He had been staring at the hanging of the mountain

67

without really seeing it. Now suddenly, in front of the precipice, there appeared the image of Lir Regan.

Giles started and almost spoke—and then she was gone.

But the vision was so real! Giles approached the hanging wondering if it was some sort of trick. He didn't want to touch the material; there was something in the texture that disturbed him. He put out his hand hesitantly but received only a slight shock from the organic quality of the cloth. Walking to one side he lifted it a little to see what was behind—and smiled. He was right, it must have been a trick. There was a door hewn out of the rock and Lir Regan must be just inside.

He slipped in back of the hanging and went through.

Then Giles stopped smiling. He was alone inside a green globe made of some unfamiliar material. There was a transparent panel on one side. A window? He approached to see. As he stepped on the center of the floor a door slid shut behind him. He whirled around, but the globe had started to spin, first slowly, then faster and faster, until he was thrown to the floor. There was a high, thin vibration, a sensation of enormous accelerating force, and then an ear-splitting explosion as the globe broke free.

Pinned heavily to the floor at that sudden upward thrust, Giles lost consciousness.

He had no idea how long he remained like that, no idea of time. When he opened his eyes he was disoriented, and his body seemed lighter in a curious way, as if he were floating or suspended. The globe was still spinning, but in a different way. Giles shook his head and groggily tried to reach out to the transparent panel. That slight motion carried and threw him against it, and then away. He saw, just briefly, what appeared to be a vast circle of blue and white, and then the globe began to rock wildly.

He fell, very suddenly, and rolled across the floor. His hand brushed against something flapping from a curve of the wall. He grabbed it and held on as the globe pitched and lurched and the spinning decreased. Then, with a savage jolt that threw him down again, it stopped. There was another muffled sound of explosion.

Giles lay head down, aching with bruises.

There was a soft sliding sound in back of him. Breathing hard, Giles found his lungs and nostrils filled with a scent that acted on him almost like a strong narcotic. He was afraid to open his eyes. He lay tense and still, breathing in that odd mixture of bittersweet and damp.

Then he began to distinguish odors and knew there were more than one. There was scent upon scent, fragrances so sharp and clean and pure that he began to cough. He pulled himself up on his knees and then stood up, dazed, to look behind him.

The curving doors had opened and beyond was a view that blinded him. He shielded his eyes and stumbled to the open door, holding to the edge for support. A wild trembling shook his body. His eyes smarted with tears and he heard himself breathing with odd choking sounds. But he had no control over his body, mind, or emotions.

He jumped to the ground in an uncoordinated movement that sent him sprawling head first. His hands flew out to dig into something dark and damp. His fingers curled around little living, bending shoots that thrust upward from the ground. His body dug into the hard but resilient turf and he breathed in the odor of earth and grass until his lungs were bursting with the richness of it. Still sobbing, he raised his head and tried to wipe his eyes. His hands were filled with the damp brown earth and his eyes burned from the contact, but he felt a fierce enjoyment of the pain. He looked up to see, rising from the earth like strange giants, huge long living limbs with leaves dancing in the wind above him and sunlight striking through branches, making pools of gold upon the ground. The green of the grass and the trees created living shadows, color and light so various that every cell in Giles's body ached with the beauty of it. He closed his eyes again, and holding his body tightly against the earth, as if he could feel its life and hear it answer, sobbed in rhythmic, passionate whispers, "Home . . . home. . . ."

He couldn't feel the earth enough. He couldn't look at the sky enough. The fleecy clouds took on strange shapes, like living creatures moving in their own blue world. The hill to his right rose in sweeping curves while the trees traced patterns against the sides. To his left a far horizon molded itself with lovely variations of hills and trees beyond a broad valley that seemed itself to be moving with the dance of long, waving grass. Giles's eyes kept filling with tears that ran unheeded down his cheeks; he didn't care, he couldn't help it. Wherever he looked there was so much life looking back. . . .

How could men have ever lived here, he wondered? How could they have existed in such a state of emotion?

The majesty of the horizon and the hills and the

70

whole broad view was too much for Giles, and he turned to a single splash of color beneath a tree.

He spent hours regarding that one flower. He looked at it from one side and then the other. He looked at it from the top and from beneath, carefully lifting the petals, afraid almost to touch them. He handled the flower as if it were something infinitely fragile and new-born. The more he looked the more he was filled with the wonder of it. His eyes were as full of awe and mystery as a child's. First one flower and then another. But they were all so different, and that became difficult. He had to rest with one thing at a time.

The sun rose high overhead, climbing above the drifting white clouds, warming his body. He couldn't look directly at it; it was so bright and dazzling. Giles moved beneath a tree to look up at the leaves in wonder, feeling the shade as a living movement around him. He spent hours like that, slowly moving his hand from the sun to the shade, watching the shadows dance on his fingers, catching a sparkle of reflection on one finger-nail and moving it so the light danced from blade to blade of grass.

He measured his hand against the grass, against a fallen leaf, against a flower petal, against a grain of earth. What size was he? What place, what relation did he have to all this? He stood up to measure his body against the tree. He touched the bark and drew his hand back quickly, still feeling the odd texture tracing his skin. He felt it again and left his hand there longer, until the bark became familiar. Then he put both arms around the trunk and his cheek against it, listening for the pulse of growth deep inside. At last he sat down

71

again and slowly leaned back, letting the tree support him.

It was as if his eyes had been so crowded with impressions that his hearing had been lost, for now, all at once, he began to hear the voices of Earth. Wind rustled the leaves above, something was singing in the air. There was a buzz, a flutter, a scraping through the bushes. As he began to take in more and more, from a distance he heard a slow rushing sound, a swirl of motion like something liquid.

Giles stood up, an expression of anticipation lighting his eyes. With his ears following the sound, his eyes seemed able to hear the unfamiliar beauty. His body, too, seemed to take its place as he walked hopefully toward the rushing, hearing it become louder.

He rounded a group of trees and there at his feet— he had almost stepped into it—was a clear, fresh stream. "A winsome curl of water winding. . . ."

If Giles could have seen himself at that moment, he would have seen man and child together, not separated by the passage of time, but merged into one. The postures and attitudes of childhood, the movements of maturity blending into one related whole. He knelt by the stream, bent his face down eagerly to drink, then tossed off his shoes and plunged in his feet with delighted satisfaction.

The water, tumbling over mossy rocks, curling in small whirlpools around fallen branches and boulders, reminded Giles that he wore more than shoes. He undressed in haste, dropping the clothes behind him, and stepped into the water. He wet himself all over, shook out his hair and waded to the middle of the stream.

There, sitting on a rock, splashing the water with wild delight, Giles observed the heap of black clothes on the bank and was reminded for the first time of Niflhel.

His face clouded as he compared the filthy garments with the green bank on which they lay. He waded back to retrieve them. He tried to wash them out, rubbing with an ancient, instinctive knowledge against a rock over which the water made a clean, swift fall. Then he arranged them in the sun to dry.

He was home.

He had known it from the moment the door of the globe opened and he had seen the face of Earth.

He had known it even before, he suspected, at that first scent of grass and ground. He needed no maps or pictures to tell him this was indeed his own, that he belonged to it and had belonged for thousands, perhaps billions of years. First his emotions, scent, and sight had told him, then his hearing, now his entire body and his mind.

The globe had transported him to Earth. How was a mystery, for there were no flying ships nor space ships on Niflhel. The ancient ones, he guessed, had truly escaped from Earth, just as the Dagda had said. But that one green globe could not have transported them all. Perhaps there was once a fleet, Giles thought. Perhaps there was still a fleet of ships on Niflhel, buried somewhere underground. Perhaps that globe was only one of many—and man could come home again!

But why hadn't the Earth Worshippers already left it that were true? They could have quietly disappeared— no, maybe not quietly. That sound of explosion when the globe accelerated—he might have burst through the surface of the planet with the force of a detonation. His foot, stepping on the floor, had seemed to accidentally trigger the departure . . . but that was strange. He had seen a vision of Lir Regan, had been so sure he would find her beyond that door. Could there be controls elsewhere that she might have used to send him here? And why? And when? He had no idea of time. . . .

How long had he been unconscious? How many years to Earth from Niflhel?

He looked up. The sun was lower and a wind was rising.

If he had caused that journey himself, accidentally, and if there were only this one globe, he might be on Earth forever, alone, with no way of return.

Return!

Giles laughed aloud while a feeling of joy surged through him. He would never return! He was *home*, and if he had to live out the rest of his life on Earth without another human being, he would never regret it. He would always have a deep sense of loss about Lir Regan, and a sorrow over those who were left behind. But he would never feel really lost or alone in his home. . . .

He felt his clothes, finding they were only slightly damp, and put them on. Before he surrendered completely to this magic of his homecoming, he would take one last look at the globe. Giles felt he owed it to those left on Niflhel. He would not step inside, but he would look carefully for some mechanism. There might be a way of sending it back again.

He took another drink from the stream and started

74

to turn back. There, in front of the leafy trees shading the bank, and watching him quietly, stood Lir Regan.

She appeared to grow out of the earth, blending with the grass and the trees as if she were one with the landscape. But this wasn't a vision—she was here, she was real. From that swift impression, Giles realized that now he couldn't visualize Earth without other men and women. Lir Regan belonged to the Earth as he did, so obviously a part that he even wondered how nature could have existed without her.

The wind lifted her hair in a waving halo and her eyes reflected the dancing light of the sun. She was incredibly beautiful, Giles thought, walking up to her and noticing her quick new smile. He responded with joy, putting aside for the moment his many questions. Far in the back of his mind was relief that there were, then, other space ships, other globes.

"I'm glad you're here," Lir Regan said simply. "I wanted you to experience Earth."

"But you called me, didn't you?" Giles said, reaching without hesitation for her hands and holding them tightly in his own. There wasn't room here for caution or subterfuge. The virgin land demanded directness and he felt a freedom that would have been incomprehensible on Niflhel. "You caused me to step behind that hanging and sent me here, didn't you?"

"Yes." She looked up at him, "I called you—in my own way. I'm sorry if it's all seemed very strange to you, Giles, but one day you'll understand."

Giles looked deeply into her eyes for a long time, aware of a completely new sensation of himself as a man toward a woman. He felt none of the old passions of Niflhel. But it was curious how, with new instincts of protection, friendship, and wonder, he sensed himself as a man more than ever before in his life. He put his arm around her and they walked to the top of a small rise beyond the grove of trees where they stood looking out at the broad expanse of valley.

"It seems to be waiting, doesn't it?" she whispered. They watched the movement of far trees bending in the wind. Low pink clouds scudded across the horizon and the sky was tinged with purple shadows that changed color as they watched.

"Look!" she pointed to a flash of color in the air, and Giles saw a winged creature streak by in an arc of blue.

His arm tightened around her shoulder. "What is it?"

"A bird," Lir Regan said. "I don't know the species, but it is a bird—a bird of Earth."

"As we are the men and women of Earth," Giles said quietly. "How did we lose it, Lir Regan? What did we do? And how is it that we are here now? How have we found it again?"

"You have already heard the story of the destruction of Earth," she answered softly, "but dead things are regenerated. Death leads into life, and Earth is living again as she waits for the homecoming of man."

Giles suddenly visualized men like the Watchers, women like Sigrid, coming home to Earth, and he shuddered.

"Not all men!" he said passionately. "Not the homecoming of *all* men!"

"No," she agreed, "And that is why you had to be here now, to understand that. Even if you had been one of us, Giles, even if you had wished to believe in

Earth, you still would not have been prepared for the reality of it. We tried, in small ways, to prepare you a little, to expose you to some of the life of Earth."

Giles nodded, understanding now why the shock of the living materials in the cave had been necessary. Without that small contact, mightn't he have collapsed altogether under the impact of the nature of Earth?

"Without that contrast between life and death," Lir Regan said, "and without actually standing here, you would never have understood why all men must not come home. Perhaps someday," she went on wistfully, "it will be for all. But now there is only the possibility for a few."

Giles thought of the globes. How many were there? How many people could be transported? And how long would it take? How far was Earth from Niflhel, and how long had he and Lir Regan been gone? Scientists were far from understanding space and time, and astronomy on Niflhel was almost totally limited by the clouds of ash that obscured the sky. If people used the globes, could they even be sure of finding Earth again. . . ?

Lir Regan seemed oblivious to these practical thoughts. Her eyes were visionary as she gazed at the hills. "Strangely enough, Giles," she said, "if you had believed in Earth you could not have been the one to play the role we hope you will. It had to be someone utterly opposed to the idea, someone who rejected it, someone so strongly entrenched in the life of Niflhel that he would even be asked to join the Watchers."

She smiled at his expression. "Yes, my uncle and I know that. We also know that you accepted, and know why. But that is what was needed. What *is* needed.

77

Someone with the capacity to understand, who would also respond to me. A skeptic who resists dreams, but could withstand the shock of having his old ideas thoroughly destroyed."

She looked up at him and said, "Someone who can accept this reality once he experiences it, and not dream that it is a dream."

Giles felt her suddenly stiffen. She looked past him with a quick, strange fear in her eyes. He whirled around, shielding her with an instinctive movement. Not five feet away stood Sigrid, her hood pulled down, her black cape grimy with soot. In her hand she held a long metallic object, and her eyes were glazed as she peered ahead.

Giles felt his heart lurch to his mouth as Lir Regan swiftly stepped in front of him and pushed him back.

"Run, Giles!" she cried. "Go back to the globe!"

He stood rigid with fear while Lir Regan urged him. "Hurry, Giles! It will be all right. Run! . . . *Giles!*"

In that last call he sensed a command so urgent that he couldn't disobey. In one word she reminded him of powers he was sure she possessed and he felt suddenly that he must do as she said.

He turned and sprinted for the globe without once looking back. He threw himself inside and heard the door slide shut. He grabbed the length of strap he had found before and managed to buckle himself in before the spinning began and the globe rocked with a violent explosion.

SEVEN

He tried to remain conscious, but when he awoke in a lifeless silence, knew he hadn't succeeded. The globe was motionless. Before he even looked toward the sliding door, Giles knew from the sensation of heavy atmosphere that he was back in Niflhel.

Even for the caves it seemed ominously silent. Giles pushed out from the hanging cautiously and found the cave empty. The robes were stacked on the floor as they had been before—no, not quite. That robe he had used himself and tossed aside, where was that? He examined the top one on the pile. Someone had been here and folded it—the Dagda perhaps? If he could only find the man he would know what to do. What did Lir Regan expect of him now?

His mind raced to answer other questions. There must be a carefully concealed opening for the globe. Something that would move aside to let it emerge from the ground, and then cover it upon return. There was no sign of debris or fallen rock, at least in here. Everything except the robe was exactly as it had been when he'd left. And when was that? How many minutes, how many years to Earth? He was afraid of the time element. He didn't understand.

Giles crawled back through the low tunnel forcing himself not to panic. He didn't want to call attention to himself by appearing on the streets of Niflhel wounded or bleeding. But did it matter? What Niflhel was he returning to? He began to wish he hadn't left the cave and the globe. He wished he hadn't obeyed Lir Regan's command. Sigrid must have chanced upon another globe—and what would Lir Regan do?

He told himself he must trust her and her mysterious power and knowledge. He had nothing else to trust except his own certainty of the reality of Earth.

Giles took a long time crawling through the tunnel and when he emerged he gasped for air. His hand brushed against something lying at the entrance. It was his own cape, he remembered now, that he'd left there. He picked it up and stood, choking. Instead of the clean fresh atmosphere there was now a regular storm of soot blowing through the empty corridors. Only a dim gray light filtered through. His feet made patterns in the film on the ground. Peering down, he saw the prints of many pairs of shoes.

Had the globe made cracks in the ground elsewhere, then, as it broke away? The force could have caused fissures in the rock above to open in places other than that secret chamber; could have brought down the dirt of Niflhel.

He walked along quickly, afraid of what he might find outside, yet anxious to know. It was so silent he could hear his own breathing. Then another faint

sound came from far down the corridor. He tensed
and jumped behind an outcropping of rock. He heard
a pattern of footsteps as silent and cautious as his own.
He didn't look around; he waited until a black cape
brushed past him. Then, with a swift leap, Giles jumped
upon the figure, pinning him to the floor, holding a hand
over his mouth.

There was a muffled cry as the man thrashed and
rolled beneath him. Then Giles saw who it was and
quickly let him go.

"I'm sorry, Master Crinan! I didn't know who it was!"
He helped him to his feet.

"Giles!" Crinan panted. "We wondered where you
were."

So he hadn't returned to Niflhel at some far point in
the future! Giles felt the shock of relief. Some incredible
mechanism within the globe cut across both space and
time. . . .

But how much time? How could he explain his
presence here beneath the Branxholm? All he could
think of was that the last time anyone had seen him was
in his imaginary pursuit of an Earth Worshipper. He
decided to risk it.

"I—I thought you were the man I was after," he said
cautiously, and held his breath until Crinan answered.

"Oh, got away, did he? Yes, I heard about that." He
tried to brush himself off but the gesture only raised
more clouds of soot from the floor. "Filthy stuff down
here," he added, peering absently down the corridor.
"Well, this area's been searched before. No point in going on. We'll forget about your man, Giles, though it's
too bad you lost him."

81

"How did you manage to locate the caves?" asked Giles as casually as he could when they started walking back in the other direction. He was hoping he hadn't led the Watchers here. He didn't think he'd been followed—and he still didn't know exactly how long ago all that had taken place. He felt an infinity of space and time between Earth and Niflhel. . . .

But Crinan said easily, "Oh, the Society's had a suspicion about the Branxholm for some time. We found a large group hidden below. Came out when we were finished with people in the city."

So they had found the Earth Worshippers! How many, Giles wondered? And why hadn't he found them himself? He should have searched further. Now he didn't know how to help or what to do. Lir Regan hadn't explained.

"So you chased your man all the way out here and kept searching," Crinan smiled. "I knew you'd be persistent, Giles."

He wondered if Crinan was testing him. "Yes—and he disappeared," Giles lied. "I got lost."

"A lot of us did," Crinan nodded in apparent sincerity. "There's a regular labyrinth of caves and tunnels here."

That must have been how Sigrid found another globe, Giles realized. If all the Watchers were searching—she might even have stumbled across the whole hidden fleet! The thought gave him a new and terrible fear. Had she been alone when she found the globe, or globes? Did anyone else know of Earth now, or of those hidden space ships? She must have stepped inside one, just as he had, and there was some scientific memory

within them that bridged these worlds. If he could return to Niflhel at almost the same point in time—so
could she. If Sigrid returned to tell the Society of
Earth's reality. . . .

There was nothing he could do to prevent it. He only
hoped that Lir Regan could. And that Sigrid had been
alone when she found it. And that she hadn't seen him
there on Earth. . . .

He would have to be very careful in maintaining his
role as a Watcher.

They came to the end of the corridor and turned into
the huge chamber where Giles had heard Lir Regan
chanting. The place bore no resemblance to that memory now. The Earth Worshippers might never have existed, or might have existed so long ago that only now
had they encroached upon an ancient meeting place.

Most of the green lights had been broken. The globes
were jagged scars against the walls. Ripped robes and
gowns and mats were strewn about the floor, heavy with
dust. The air was foul.

"Come along." Crinan started slowly across the chamber.

There was something queer about his movements.
Even at ordinary walking pace Giles would have out-
distanced him easily. Crinan was beginning to act like
a man just roused from a deep sleep. He stumbled a
little.

"Is something the matter?" asked Giles. He noticed
that Crinan seemed hardly aware of the bruise on his
cheek where he'd fallen, although it was turning an
ugly red.

"No, just the air, I think. Can't seem to breathe very

well." He started choking and leaned on Giles for support as they headed toward a flight of stairs.

The steps, hewn out of the rough rock, were well lit with a string of glaring white lights, evidently put there by the Watchers. Giles helped Crinan up with difficulty and pushed against the door at the top. It swung open and Crinan pitched forward, gasping for breath.

They were in the large, round dome of the Branxholm. Here the air was cleaner. A low vibration came from air purifiers that had been hastily hooked up, and from the spotlights that played over every curve of the vast enclosure. The glare from the revolving lights was blinding, and it took Giles a few moments to see what had been done.

Far across the room a line of Watchers stood in a semicircle guarding the group of Earth Worshippers who were each placed a precise distance from the other against the curving wall. They were still dressed in the colorful, softly flowing clothes of their underground meetings. The color, against the black border of Watcher guards, was like a capsuled impression of life and death, of Earth and Niflhel.

Giles looked quickly and figured there must be one guard for every two Earth Worshippers. All were perfectly still. The Watchers had their hands on their hips ready for any sudden movement. Then Giles frowned furiously. There were a number of children there, standing rigidly and afraid. In their colorful garments they looked like small stiff flowers, pressed against the wall.

He turned to Crinan angrily, "They're holding the children! Is that necessary?"

"I know, but I'm sure it's not for long, Giles. Just a

temporary measure." He took a deep breath and seemed to recover a little in the cleaner air. "They'll be released, I'm sure."

"*When?*" Giles demanded.

"There's nothing we can do about it! They'll be released when the questioning is over. Now come along, Giles!"

Perhaps Master Crinan believed this, but Giles knew better. No "questioning" was even going on. How could the man not at least protest to someone? And he'd been so anxious to have children of his own. Giles held back for a moment, looking for a way to help. But he had no authority, not even direction from Lir Regan or the Dagda—and Crinan was urging him to the exit.

A guard opened the door for them and they were outside.

The soot hung like black flakes in an odd half-light. Was it dawn or dusk on Niflhel? Would it be dawn or dusk on Earth for Lir Regan—and perhaps Sigrid? The question of time still bothered Giles and he tried to reconstruct. It had been after midnight when Sigrid came to his door; time had passed at the street barricade; he had spent hours in the cave of the hangings and felt it was nearly dawn. And then—he had entered the globe and it seemed as if he had spent an entire day on Earth. Hadn't the sun been setting? It had been a magical pink and purple world when Sigrid had appeared. . . .

Did this mean that an entire day had passed on Niflhel as well? How long had those people been standing? It could have been a day or only an hour or two. There was nothing in the overcast sky and strange half-light to give him any real indication.

Crinan walked to a metallic shed that had been erected against the side of the building. To his surprise, Giles saw that the buried tracks had been uncovered and the old Gondola was in operation again. That had taken time! They couldn't have managed to do this within an hour or two. Possibly a day had passed.

They sat down in bucket seats facing each other. The guard released the brake, and the wagon sped off along the tracks, rocking toward the City. The same old Gondola! Giles looked out the window and felt a sudden onslaught of nostalgia. He observed the emotion with amazement. If he could have such feelings about his childhood and youth on Niflhel, what would impressions of Earth be like for a child born there? The impact of the idea, and the possibilities strained his greatest imagination.

Even Master Crinan seemed to be experiencing something similar. He looked inside and outside the Gondola and murmured, "So strange to be here again. . . ." Then he became silent and closed his eyes.

Where was Crinan taking him, Giles wondered? He couldn't ask—as a Watcher he would only follow.

Crinan seemed to be asleep, or back in that curious, dreamlike state. He slumped in his seat, head hanging down, eyes tightly closed.

When the wagon stopped, Giles had to help him off. Crinan coughed again and shook his head as if trying to clear his vision. "Sorry. The ride must have made me dizzy. I'll be all right."

They stepped out to a platform at the last street of Niflhel. Directly ahead was the end of the Underground. Crinan held on to Giles as they descended the elevator. A tube was approaching, and when it stopped Giles helped Crinan into an empty alcove. He was still having trouble with his eyes, opening and closing them.

"Look here, Master Crinan," said Giles, genuinely worried. "I don't think you're in any condition to travel."

"No, I have orders!" Crinan returned sharply. The words awakened him and he sat up straight as the tube whined away. "Most important. Head of the Society wants to see you—expecting you. Have to go directly to Headquarters."

Society Headquarters! Giles felt a sudden panic. Had Sigrid returned, then, to tell them of Earth? Or of seeing him there?

"You'll have to keep me going," Crinan mumbled. "Keep me moving."

"I could go alone," Giles urged quickly. If Crinan would only tell him where the Headquarters was located he could choose his own time about going there. He needed time to think, to anticipate what might be said. Even if Sigrid had returned to report, he wasn't positive she had seen him. Lir Regan had stepped so quickly between them, and Sigrid had looked so dazed. . . .

"Tell me where to go," Giles insisted. "I'll go on myself."

Crinan laughed shortly. "Sorry, Giles—orders."

The tube stopped at a station. Crinan rose and exited with astonishing speed. Giles had to admire his effort, the man was so obviously ill. This time they took the stairs halfway up, and then Crinan stopped to look around carefully. No one was in sight. He ran his hand over the blocks of stone on the stairwell, then pressed, and a part of the wall swung open. With a hurried exclamation, he drew Giles through. The wall shut behind them.

They were in another tunnel. Giles was now amazed at what he guessed must be an entire honeycomb of underground passages beneath all Niflhel. And who knew of the existence of this network? Earth Worshippers? The Society of the Protectors? Did one know of the other's location?

He followed Crinan until the tunnel made a sharp turn. There Crinan opened a door and they stepped into an elevator that descended swiftly. In a moment the doors opened on another network of corridors. But these walls were smooth and blank and brightly lit and the air was clean. They walked past a series of numbered doors until Crinan stopped before the one door with no marking on it. He spoke into a disk on the side, "Bran Crinan here."

Instantly the door opened. And Giles gasped as he stepped into what must have been the most vulgar and most luxurious room in all of Niflhel.

Unlike the peaceful effect of the exposure to green in the loft and the caves, the colors in this room shocked the senses. The lights were harsh and brilliant—purple, scarlet, blinding reds and blues. The walls were decorated in the same hard colors with murals of an idealized Niflhel. And these murals acted as frames for the largest mirrors Giles had ever seen. The reflection made the room seem to stretch on endlessly. The rug was inches thick. Giles sank in it, and looking down, saw that of all things, the rug was white. Pure, frigid, antiseptic white. Whiter than his graduation cloak or Lir Regan's gown. . . .

The lurid colors and the mirrors had distracted him from noticing an enormous desk at the end of the room. But then a voice screamed at them that made the hair on the back of his neck bristle. A figure was leaning forward from the desk, cursing them for not removing their capes and shoes, for dirtying his rug.

Giles smiled coolly and deliberately unfastened his cape, letting it fall with a shower of more soot on the rug. He felt exactly as he had three years before. He knew by the voice, before he even looked closer, who was sitting behind that desk, and he felt a surge of anticipation.

His old classmate, Car Saunders, looked from the heap of black on the rug up to Giles's face. He hesitated exactly as he had three years ago on Examination Day. Then he rose from his seat and came forward, smiling. "Hello, Giles, come in."

EIGHT

"Hello, Saunders."

Giles walked slowly toward the desk. In a strange
way he wasn't surprised to find his old adversary here.
There was something weirdly fitting about it. He took
the outstretched hand distastefully, seeing how the boy
he remembered had changed. Car Saunders had grown
old. His hair was receding, and his face was flabby and
mottled, as if he relied too much on stimulants. They
were the same age but Saunders looked years older than
Giles.

"Good to see you, Chulainn. Sorry to shout like that,
but Master Crinan should have taken you to the shower
first. I guess he can't keep his mind on details." Saunders
was painfully polite.

Bran Crinan had slumped into the nearest chair without bothering to remove his cape. His head hung down
and he was breathing heavily. Giles was worried about
him. "He seems to be ill, Saunders. He had a difficult
time getting me here. I think someone should take a
look—"

"What about that, Crinan?" Car Saunders walked over to smile at him. "Giles Chulainn here thinks you need some attention."

"Yes, please," Crinan mumbled distantly. "Just need to lie down perhaps—"

Saunders kicked him angrily, "Wake up, Crinan!"

The man looked up with glazed eyes for a moment and then slumped again. Giles took a step forward, but Saunders waved him away. He looked down at Crinan and said to Giles. "In case you're wondering why I'm here, know that I'm the man you're working for. I'm the Head of Watchers for the Society."

He kept staring at Crinan and went on. "There you have a picture of a man who didn't know what side he was on. Take this in, Giles, look at him and remember. We asked Crinan to join us primarily because you were working under him, and for certain reasons, we wanted you. But Crinan never reported a little journey he made several years ago. That was his mistake. Naturally we knew of it and waited for him to tell us of his own accord. But he never did, so of course we know he can't be trusted—"

Master Crinan suddenly lurched to his feet. He would have fallen but Giles swiftly caught him. Car Saunders ignored the episode.

"Something had to be done. Crinan fulfilled his major duty of bringing you in, and here, but he obviously isn't fit for anything further. He'll be quite comfortable now, though, I assure you." Saunders walked swiftly to his desk and pushed a button.

Immediately one of the mirrors on the wall slid back to reveal a door. Two men dressed in white suits and hoods came in. Crinan was still slumped against Giles. He knew it would be futile to resist. The men lifted Master Crinan and removed him; the mirror slid back into place. Except for the black ash and soot in the chair, Bran Crinan might never have existed. Giles knew he would never see him again.

He stared at Car Saunders blankly and his thoughts flew to Laeg Falkirk—the Head of *their* school. Was this what happened to Falkirk? Used, drugged—in his case questioned, as Sigrid had said—and then quietly removed? But there was something very wrong here. Maybe Falkirk had been a secret Earth Worshipper, but he was sure Bran Crinan hadn't. Even if he had attended one meeting, as Saunders had hinted, Bran Crinan was absolutely loyal to Niflhel. . . .

With a shrinking feeling, Giles wondered if this entire event had been "staged" only for him?

Saunders laughed in a high, disconnected giggle. It was revolting and Giles clenched his fists, wanting to slam him to the floor. Only thoughts of Lir Regan prevented him. Her only hope, and the Dagda's, and the rest of the Earth Worshippers' lay in his maintaining a perfect posture in his role of Watcher.

Still laughing, Saunders sat behind his desk and gestured to a seat in front. Giles walked forward stiffly and sat down. Saunders withdrew a handkerchief from his pocket and wiped his eyes. "He'd forgotten all about that one meeting he attended, I think," said Saunders. "Knew it wasn't even worth mentioning. Or knew that we knew—it didn't matter. But it was an excuse and things have to be done this way sometimes."

He grinned at Giles. "Remember that."

His fingers drummed loosely on the desk as he looked

at Giles. Giles watched the fingers idly drumming—and then he saw the paperweight.

He felt the color drain from his face and held his breath—

The paperweight—

It was a small, round ball, flattened on the bottom and accurately etched above in blue and green with the outlines of the seas and continents of Earth.

A small globe of Earth.

Watching him, Saunders casually picked up the globe. He rolled it in his hand. Then with a quick motion, he tossed it. "Catch!" he cried, still grinning.

Giles leaped and caught it—it was warm with the dampness of Saunders's palms.

Saunders smiled with a private joke. "Of course you don't believe in Earth, do you, Giles Chulainn?"

Giles looked down at the globe in his hand, feeling sick. Whatever he answered was sure to be wrong. His forefinger traced the edge of a continent, just a line on a small, hard ball. Something changed within him. Could it all have been a dream? Perhaps his feet had never touched a grassy hill on Earth, had never felt that winding stream—perhaps he should tell all this to Saunders. His safety—even the safety of others—might lie right here, rather than in this "dream" he cupped in his hand. His fingers tightened round the globe as he remembered something Lir Regan had said. . . .

". . . someone who could accept this reality once he'd experienced it, and not dream that it was a dream. . . ."

Dream that it was a dream. He became very dizzy for a moment, and then it passed. And then Giles saw, as if they were standing in this room, that line of people against the walls of the Branxholm. He saw the children standing motionless until this man chose to release them.

Giles replaced the paperweight carefully on the desk. Dream or reality, he must go on in the only way he knew, as Watcher, and continue to deny Earth.

"No, I don't believe in Earth," he said steadily to Car Saunders. "Would I be here if I did?"

Saunders tapped the globe. "But you've seen this before?"

"Of course. There was a larger globe at the meeting I attended."

"Yes, we have them, too." Saunders's smile faded. "But you're very dense, Giles, if the reality of all this has escaped you. Naturally Earth exists! A legend like that doesn't grow out of nothing. It's hard to believe you didn't suspect—you've had enough exposure."

Giles was stunned at the open disclosure.

"Earth does exist!" Saunders insisted. "I don't care what your feelings are or what your education has been. You'll have to revise all that. Earth exists. The planet is as real as Niflhel!"

He looked at Giles narrowly to see how he was taking it. Giles could only nod, stupidly.

"Once that's clear you must understand the knowledge is secret. Not to be disclosed to anyone. Without exception! Is that understood?"

"Yes, of course," said Giles slowly.

"For certain reasons you must know," Saunders went on, "but your future will depend on how well you keep this secret."

The warning was obvious. The memory of Bran Crinan was still in the room. Giles nodded again.

"There's more," said Saunders. "I don't have to tell you why our history has been rewritten. If we had known of the existence of Earth in school, would either of us have been content with Niflhel? This is why the knowledge has been so well guarded within the Society."

"Sigrid knows, doesn't she?" Giles felt he had to ask that question.

"No, she doesn't!" Saunders replied sharply. "And she mustn't. Only a few key people know."

Then she hadn't returned from Earth, thought Giles, or she would surely have reported to him. She must still be there, with Lir Regan.

"We didn't mind the religion of Earth," Saunders continued, "as long as the Earth Worshippers confined their activities to the meetings and rituals. It was actually a help to us, a screen for our activities. But the recent interest, the numbers of new people—that had to be curbed. The thing was starting to become too real. Too many intelligent people getting involved. Someone might have guessed—"

He rose from his seat and began pacing the room. "Ironically enough, it's the Earth Worshippers themselves who haven't believed in the reality of their dream! Think about that, Giles, and you'll see what sort of people they are. . . ."

He muttered, speaking more to himself than to Giles. "And all of us can't get there. Has to be the ones who can create a new civilization from a wilderness. The builders—the architects of a new world."

Saunders stopped shortly. His eyes narrowed as he turned to Giles, as if he were deciding upon something. For a time there was absolute silence in the room. Then he began to speak in a quick whisper.

95

"And *you* never wondered why you were building new roads, digging new mines? For more industry, you thought, more mines for more factories. Didn't it ever occur to you that all these roads, and mines, are unnecessary? Did you ever compare them to the population of Niflhel?"

Giles frowned and Saunders laughed. "You never knew you were looking for Earth, did you?"

Giles rose to his feet, staring.

"Yes! You were looking for the lost fleet of ships that brought us here in the beginning! We know they exist. They have to. How else could man have come here?"

They even knew of the ships!

"A fleet of space ships thousands of years old," Car Saunders went on, "but without them Earth will be lost, and we will be lost forever! Giles! Didn't you ever wonder what might be beyond this filthy haze? With all our advanced technology we can't look into the universe. But there are the secrets—the instruments, the navigation to lead us, blind as we are, off this hellish planet. And in all these thousands of years we haven't been able to find one ship."

Saunders walked back to his desk and sagged down in the chair. "We thought they might have been destroyed," he said. "Men may have needed whatever power there was on those ships to create sources of light and energy here in the beginning. But we felt they would have left at least one ship! They wouldn't destroy all records, leaving us with no way of return. So while looking for the lost fleet, we were also searching for *one* hidden ship.

"When we discovered the caves under the Branxholm, we thought it might be hidden there. And we were right."

Giles tried to keep his face expressionless. He didn't know what was coming next, but his old classmate surprised him.

"We didn't find an actual ship in the Branxholm—we found something else, perhaps more important. After all these years, Giles, we discovered that there is a torch bearer who has real information of all the secrets. Who knows where the ship, or fleet of ships, is hidden, and how to use them. Throughout centuries this information has been passed down to certain persons among the Earth Worshippers. In other words, a few key people among them, as well, also know that Earth is real! Sit down!"

Giles had been standing in front of Saunders's desk, hardly breathing. *Why* was the man telling him all this? It was information only for the Society of Protectors. He sank down apprehensively, waiting.

"This is why we need you, Giles," Saunders said. "Sigrid has wanted you in the Society for a long time; she's had you watched, we know your activities. We know that you have taken an interest in a certain girl among these people, and she is interested in you.

"You are to find her! She has disappeared—and she is the current torch bearer, the keeper of the secrets, the one they call the Bard. She is the niece of an old man called the Dagda.

"You are to find that girl! And through her discover where the ship, or ships, are hidden. I am going to release her uncle in your custody as a decoy—"

"You have him?" asked Giles in a whisper.

"We have him," Saunders smiled coldly. "And between you, you're bound to find her. Once you have that old man in your custody, Giles, you're to act like an Earth Worshipper and pretend you never heard of the Society! You profess to be a Watcher now, and you'll have to work that out."

Giles tried to suppress sudden elation. The Dagda! The old man could tell him what to do.

Saunders smiled again. "No matter what you think your game is, Giles, remember there'll be someone watching you. Remember your teacher, Master Bran Crinan. And remember this, too, if you should happen to have any notion of sympathy for the Earth Worshippers . . . and if you have any dreams of Earth yourself.

"Repairing and using—or rebuilding a fleet of space ships requires more than a group of empty-headed dreamers. It takes scientists and mathematicians and any number of specially qualified men. We have them. Earth Worshippers don't. With us you might get there. Without us, you won't. I suggest you act most carefully."

He lifted the paperweight from a pile of plastic sheets and glanced at Giles with amusement before he started writing.

"Here," he handed the paper to Giles. "Your authorization for the Dagda's release. I feel better, Giles. I feel we're on the right track at last."

"And when and if you do find the ships," said Giles, fingering the paper in his hand, "what do you intend to do? Will you transport everyone from Niflhel gradually? Evacuate the planet?"

Saunders's smile broadened to a grin. "What do you think?"

Giles looked at him without answering.

Saunders laughed and waved a hand expansively. "Oh, eventually perhaps everyone would be evacuated —as you put it. But after all, we would have to create a beginning—as we did here. We might first need to transport materials—the fruits of our years of industry here."

Giles nodded, understanding quite well. The masters on Earth would be served by the slaves of Niflhel. The picture was crystal clear. A fleet of ships transporting goods and luxuries mined and fabricated on Niflhel by a swarm of workers who would work out their lives with a dream of one day reaching Earth themselves.

He looked off at a point beyond Saunders's head, visualizing the sort of "civilization" the Society of Protectors would build over the valleys and the warm green hills of Earth. But the vision was obscured with a gray ash and a dark, leaden sky. Some words the Dagda had read recurred to Giles. . . .

And it was corrupt, for all flesh had corrupted their way upon the earth. . . .

His eyes came back to Saunders's. Giles tried to look, too, as if he were luxuriating in that same, corrupt dream.

"I think we understand each other, Giles," Saunders smiled. "Just remember that you're in the middle of another Examination. I hope it goes better for you than the last."

NINE

Once out in the hall, Giles's first thought was for his teacher, Master Bran Crinan. He found it difficult to go on without looking for him. But past this corridor there were countless others and hundreds of doors . . . even if he did succeed in finding Crinan, what could he do? No man deserved a fate like this, no matter what he'd done. And what had Crinan done? Nothing, except grow old too rapidly, become too lonely, and out of weakness join the Society. Giles had a feeling of deep sorrow about the man whom he had once trusted and liked so much, but sadly gave up the idea of helping him. The task was impossible, and there were other tasks ahead.

He didn't know where to begin! At the thought of possible choices confronting him, Giles felt his mind as a labyrinth comparable to the web of tunnels under Niflhel. Had anyone ever been given so many different tastes of truth with so little certainty about any of them? And to meet Car Saunders as Head of the Watchers . . . he wondered at the meaning of that. There was something too classical, beyond chance or accident about it. He felt as if a master designer had been working at a serious and complicated game, and he was a piece moving across the board. At the same time the mysterious understanding that this was more than a game haunted him. The map was drawn, several avenues were open, but now he would have to move of his own choice. And where was the true road to Earth?

He entered the elevator and reached the surface quickly. But the door in the wall took some time to open. Giles stood before it looking without success for some mechanism. Then it suddenly slid back and he stepped into the Underground stairwell. He understood —it opened only when the steps were free of people.

He was still holding the paper of authorization in his hand. He looked at it before tucking it away under his cape. The Dagda was being held at the Branxholm— strange that he hadn't noticed him standing with the others against the wall. No, Giles realized, they would have kept the old man apart from the others. He frowned, wondering if the Dagda had been subjected to extreme measures of questioning.

Giles decided that he didn't want to pick him up just yet. It could be the very worst thing; it could be a trick. He wanted a chance to look at all he had learned, the weird series of possibilities. What was the logical thing to do? As a sincere Watcher, his first move would be to go directly to the Branxholm—but couldn't he first pause at home? Anyone following would assume he wished to shower and change; a reasonable respite, Giles thought, before attempting to "find that girl". . . .

Under his hood, Giles smiled grimly. He would lead

his Watcher a long way out of the way before finally reaching the Branxholm. He turned abruptly at the corner and went to the next Underground.

A stream of people was emerging from the shaft—workers about to start their day. Giles threaded his way down through the black-caped crowd and got on an empty tube returning to the city's residential area. His Watcher, whoever he was, was doing a fine job of remaining invisible. As far as Giles saw he was entirely alone in the tube. He leaned back and a wave of exhaustion flooded through him. He hadn't realized he was so tired. He closed his eyes, but tried to remain awake while green images of Earth swam before him. Once home he would have to take something. . . .

The streets were deserted when he got off, and as he walked back to his hut under the steaming heat of the hazy sky, he tried to catalog what he had learned. Each fact had after it a question.

The Society knew of Earth. But how much did they know and where had they received their knowledge? How many of the Protectors were aware of Earth's reality?

Giles wondered if Saunders himself was the only one who knew. It was possible.

Another thought had disturbed him earlier—Car Saunders might not be sure of Earth at all. He might merely suspect, and be using Giles as some sort of decoy to discover whether or not it were true.

He wanted Lir Regan—*why, really?* To lead them to that fleet of ships, or only to confirm the existence of Earth?

Maybe what Saunders had said about that lost fleet

was a pretext altogether! Maybe the Society had already found those ships, had sent Sigrid there. Maybe they were already occupying Earth!

Giles stopped short, thinking about that. It would explain Sigrid's presence in a different way. It would explain why they had so suddenly Classified the Earth Worshippers. If, as Saunders said, more intelligent people were taking an interest in the groups, they would have to stop any real search in fear the Earth Worshippers would actually find their "dream."

He felt sick. Had he been living in a fool's paradise all this time, working on his roads at the frontiers of this miserable world while men like Saunders were already enjoying the air and wind and water of Earth?

No, there was something wrong in the thought. He had smelled the rich damp ground of home. He had felt the clean wind and seen the pure, clean sky. He had held Lir Regan's hands as if they were both Earth's new children. . . . No, he couldn't have stood on Earth so freely if it had been defiled with the presence of men like Saunders. He would have felt it, and certainly Lir Regan would have known, if a civilization of Saunders's making were halfway round the globe.

He plodded on to his hut, bone tired, sick of the ash that blanketed him, sick of the smell of smoke and taste of grime.

He was left with more questions. If all of Saunders's story were true, what would happen once he picked up the Dagda? What would they do with Lir Regan if she returned? And if Sigrid had actually found the fleet of ships and returned first. . . .

He turned up the walk to his hut thinking that everything depended, really, on what had happened between Sigrid and Lir Regan. He opened the door and went directly into the shower room.

After the jets had cleansed him, Giles looked in his closet for a pill to keep awake. He swallowed it dry. Then, thinking of the liquid stream on Earth, angrily ran several full cups of water and drank them all. His ration was gone, but wide awake now, he didn't care. He felt a savage desire to return to that fair green planet alone, without anyone, even the Dagda. To return naked if possible and stand on the hills of Earth as if newborn.

He caught a glimpse of himself in the mirror and his expression startled him. His face was pale, the faint freckles stood out starkly and his red-blond hair, clean from the shower, leaped around his face like a flame. He ran a comb through it quickly, trying to subdue the violence in his eyes. This was not how a man should look—wild and slightly hysterical; he was not fit for anything in this state. He looked almost as Sigrid had looked when she faced Lir Regan. He would have to collect himself, Giles thought, turning away from the mirror. Regardless of events or his questions, he would have to be calmer before he went for the Dagda.

He entered his bedroom.

It was dirty. His bare feet felt soot on the floor. He looked at his bed with a sharp intake of breath but tried to keep his face expressionless. Sigrid hadn't bothered to remove her cape. She had propped up the pillows and lay against them, the black cloak spreading grotesque wings across the cover. Under the mass of her streaming gold hair, her eyes, piercing into his, were filled with suspicion.

She smiled. The contradiction was so violent that Giles couldn't respond.

"Welcome home, Giles," said Sigrid.

He stared, sensing her extreme hostility. But he mustn't let his emotions show. Giles forced himself to smile and hold back the questions that filled him, making his heart pound. Had she seen him on Earth and had she been to Saunders yet?

Instead he heard himself saying softly, "Sigrid." And then he walked toward the bed as he had done so many times before. He thought what an incredible memory the body had of its own past movements. The imitation was faultless. Perhaps in this capacity to imitate himself lay some enormous source of power—and of hope. He must continue, and retrace himself again to where he had last seen Sigrid.

Watching him, her eyes widened in surprise, and some of the hostility vanished. "Giles—I thought—"

"That I had run off without you?" His smile deepened. "But you remember, I had a man to pursue. I thought you would follow."

"But I did." She was bewildered. "I followed with the others until we all lost you. And then later, after we discovered the Branxholm, I was sure you'd chased him there—but I couldn't find you."

"Were you there when they found the Earth Worshippers?" asked Giles.

Sigrid frowned. "Of course. Weren't you?"

"Yes, but lower down," Giles answered quickly. "I thought I had him and I kept looking. There's a labyrinth of tunnels, you know. As a matter of fact I got lost." He sat on the bed beside her and began softly stroking her hair. "Where were you?"

Sigrid looked at him with relief. "Oh, then that's it
. . . I was with the guards upstairs, at least for a
while." She closed her eyes and a faint line appeared
again on her forehead. She turned her head away from
him. "But then I think I must have been lost myself.
I can't quite remember. Please don't do that, Giles."

She moved his hand away from her hair and with a
quick movement sat straight up in the bed, frowning as
she tried to explain. "They were having a service down
below when we found them," she said carefully. "The
old man was leading them. Didn't you see that?"

She looked at him quickly but Giles shook his head.

Sigrid considered that for a moment. "Then there
must be another way down; I don't understand."

Giles watched her tensely. She seemed to be, for the
first time he could remember, on the defensive. She was
hesitant and cautious.

"They were singing something—I don't know the
words—and they had that green globe hanging in back
of the leader." Sigrid looked down and clasped her
hands tightly together. Then she looked up and ap-
pealed to him again. "You must have heard it, Giles."

"No, I didn't," he said flatly.

"Well, the rest of us did and it was such a shock at
first that we just watched for a while." She shrugged,
"After all, they were all there. It was a mistake to look
for them in the city. We'd found the main group and
there was plenty of time. No way for them to escape."
She gave a short laugh.

But Giles sensed, under that brittle smile, an under-
current of doubt. An odd thought struck him—could
Sigrid, of all people, have been affected by that meeting?

She destroyed that idea immediately. "Such a childish religion," she said contemptuously. "Silly people, idiotic ideas. I can't imagine why. . . ." Her voice trailed off and she asked Giles nervously, "Do you think it possible that they use some form of mass hypnosis? Or have some mechanical means of inducing dreams?"

"I have no idea," Giles quickened with hope at her words.

"That must be it," she said, "because it's the only thing that could explain—well—I think I can tell you. I had a strange dream that I saw Earth."

Giles laughed, a bit unsteadily.

"No, it's true," said Sigrid seriously. "They must have some way of projecting that imaginary picture. Terribly dangerous. For a moment I was certain I was standing on Earth, and the colors, the images—if such a planet existed—"

Giles no longer heard what she was saying. His heart was pounding so furiously he was sure Sigrid must notice. She had given him the answer—she thought she had dreamed it! Lir Regan could be responsible, could have hypnotized her. Unless. . . .

He rose from the bed abruptly and paced across the room, keeping his face averted. Unless Sigrid was lying about everything. He remembered the weapon she held in her hand when she was near Lir Regan. Giles whirled around. Sigrid lay on the bed smiling, and then, meeting his eyes, she got up quickly amid a shower of soot from the cape. The covers were empty. There was no weapon there. It could be concealed in her cape. Giles crossed the room swiftly and took her in his arms, heedless of the dirt. He held her closely until he knew that she was concealing nothing. She could have dropped it on Earth then, or anywhere while in her "dream." She could have harmed Lir Regan.

She drew back and whispered, "I'd love to stay, Giles, but this time I can't. Crinan is waiting for us at the Branxholm, and once we arrive the Judgments can start."

It was like a sharp blow. Judgments for the Earth Worshippers—she couldn't mean it!

"We've never used Judgments for any group of people," he said, trying to conceal his fear. "Only for individuals who threatened security, and that was centuries ago."

"Of course," Sigrid smiled, "but what would you call these people except individuals who threaten security? How silly, Giles. Naturally, they're all traitors."

"They've made no real disturbance," Giles said doggedly.

"Of course they have," her eyes narrowed. "Everyone has been disturbed."

"They've not harmed anyone," Giles insisted, "and that was the only basis of law for invoking the use of Judgments."

"They have harmed me!" Sigrid replied sharply. "Showing me a picture of something that doesn't exist, upsetting my natural process of discrimination. It's like an unlawful use of narcotics. I didn't request a picture of Earth; I didn't ask for a dream!"

There was something so convincing in her tone that Giles thought she had been telling the truth. And she had also mentioned Crinan, waiting at the Branxholm. . . .

"Master Crinan isn't waiting any longer," said Giles, watching her expression. "He was very ill, in fact, when we went to see Saunders."

His name seemed to surprise her. "So you've met Car Saunders again—"

"Didn't he tell you?" Giles watched her intently.

"No—I haven't seen him since—since—" She broke off.

Giles felt it might be true. Perhaps she had been afraid to face him after her experience. But whether or not she was telling the truth, she had seen Earth. She had found a globe. Even if she thought she had dreamed it, how long would it be before she decided to speak to Saunders about it? How long before she might realize it had not been a dream?

Quickly, Giles went to the dressing room for his clothes. He would have to keep her with him every minute. She must be by his side until he knew what to do.

He was terrified at her disclosure of the Judgments. For the Earth Worshippers it could mean only one thing. They would be mercilessly exterminated as some heretical groups had been centuries ago. To Giles's knowledge, the law of Judgments was an anachronism, something frightening that one read about in history, some unbelievable error in the beginnings of man's attempt to build a stable society on Niflhel. It didn't seem possible that such brutality could be unleashed now in the sophisticated order of the day. He wanted to believe that Sigrid was wrong, that she had made a terrible mistake. But her attitude of unconcern, her complete acceptance of the old law told him otherwise.

109

Giles wondered whether unknown to himself and to the rest of Niflhel, the law had been quietly invoked before. Who knew what secret courts might have met? Who knew what actually happened to those Classified Contrary, to people like Falkirk and Bran Crinan? One heard grim hints from time to time, but they were quickly forgotten in the pursuit of one's own activities.

The Hierarchy of Niflhel, the government—were they truly a group of fine men, leading their citizens, or was the government merely a facade, taking their orders from the Society of Protectors? Giles wished he had paid more attention to those relatives of his own who had been active in government. He wished he had dug more deeply into the archives that contained the history of the families of Niflhel. He wished he had asked his parents about it before they died.

His grandmother—he saw her again standing bareheaded before her hut, raising her hands to the sky. She had known, Giles was sure, She had *known,* and if only he had listened. He caught again the echo of her voice saying, "If we were standing on Earth, Giles. . . ."

She had said it almost as if it were possible. Giles felt a rush of tenderness toward the memory of that bent, gray-haired figure who had never realized her dream. She had been, perhaps without ever admitting it, another Earth Worshipper, another visionary.

With startling quickness, as if a veil had been suddenly lifted, Giles began to see. How could he have been so blind! Until now he himself had thought of the Earth Worshippers as visionary dreamers, fanatics, even fools. His own fantastic journey to Earth, in retrospect, had seemed dreamlike—and worse—as something only

110

for himself and Lir Regan. His attitude had been exclusive, really, in the deepest sense. He had been touched largely by ideas, not by the flesh-and-blood facts of real people facing perverted minds. For the Watchers, the Society, yes all of Niflhel, was perverted in a way he was just beginning to understand.

When he returned to his bedroom he looked into Sigrid's eyes and saw there the same perversion, the same blank acceptance, the same living death he had seen during the soot-filled night of the detentions. . . .

Giles felt a sick wave of remorse. Not dreamers—no! The Earth Worshippers were the only *real* people in Niflhel. Whether they knew the reality of their dream, however they regarded Earth—as a myth or some unobtainable heaven or some ancient memory—an instinctive part of them had rightly rejected the evil of Niflhel. They were not dreamers and fools! They were intuitively wise people who had reached the great question of where man belonged.

How brave they were to maintain that question. And now they stood there at the Branxholm, waiting . . . and somehow their fate was linked to his, as was his to theirs. No matter what might have happened to Lir Regan, Giles knew he was no longer alone.

"We'd better go," he said to Sigrid softly.

He put on his cape and they left the hut.

111

TEN

They had thrown a cordon of armed Watchers around the Branxholm. The black-hooded figures stood at rigid intervals like an army of statues, the only movement being the lift and fall of their capes in the gusts of wind and soot. Giles helped Sigrid out of the Gondola and looked up. The atmosphere was a dirty, dark brown. Far away along the horizon was a cloud of darkness stretching as far as he could see.

He paused for a moment on the platform. Although he had seen many dust storms on Niflhel, there was something unusually ominous about that cloud of black that now looked so still and far away. But distances were not what they seemed. As the cloud advanced across the flats it would gather more and more ash, growing gradually larger, until, by the time it reached the city, all Niflhel would be engulfed. As a child he had almost enjoyed the dust storms. It was different and exciting to huddle inside wondering what he would see when the storm was past.

Sigrid followed his glance and shivered slightly. "It looks like a bad one."

"How long before it's due, do you know?" Giles asked the nearest guard.

Under his hood and visor the Watcher's voice was muffled. "They say several hours but it's not certain."

"It's never certain," Giles agreed. He took Sigrid's arm and led her to the doors.

All during their ride from the city he had wondered how to extract real information from her. He was tired of surmises and wild guesses. He was still unsure whether her story was the truth or a lie, and if she had already reported to Saunders. But he was afraid to question too much. If the truth, he didn't want to remind her of that "lost" time when she had "dreamed" of Earth.

Inside the large hall the people were still standing. How long had it been by now? The children leaned against the wall, arms outstretched on either side, legs trembling. The adults stood out from the wall with no support. Two of them had fallen in a faint to the floor.

Beside him, Sigrid laughed a little at the scene. Giles gripped her arm tightly and walked across the hall to a guard standing alone in the center. He wore a special marking on his cape and seemed to be in charge.

"Let them sit down," Giles ordered.

Both the guard and Sigrid stared at him in surprise.

"Your name?" Giles asked the guard sharply.

"Duncan," he said hesitantly. Then, as Giles's face hardened, he abruptly barked out the order. One by one, as it was repeated by the other guards, the Earth Worshippers slowly sank down.

"What do you think you're doing, Giles?" Sigrid whispered, frowning.

"Following my instructions from Car Saunders," he said coldly. He whipped out the paper of authorization and showed it to Duncan, who with a respectful nod, motioned Giles to follow.

"That wasn't part of your instructions, was it?" asked Sigrid as they walked down the stairs to the caverns.

"Using my own judgment is," said Giles.

They had put the Dagda in a small, rough cavern on a lower level. One Watcher stood outside the jagged entrance. As his eyes became accustomed to the dim light, Giles saw that the Dagda was standing quite still in the center of the room, his head upright, his eyes closed.

"Release him in this man's custody," Duncan showed the authorization to the guard. "You're relieved now."

The guard yawned appreciatively and waved toward the Dagda. "Get him to move if you can. I had orders to let him sit down but he insists upon standing like that. Refused every bit of food or water. I'm glad to have someone else try." He yawned again and with a doubtful shrug at Giles, walked off.

Duncan looked inside and told the Dagda, "You're released in the custody of Giles Chulainn."

There was no response. Duncan frowned and tried again, louder, "You may come out now!"

The old man didn't move or open his eyes.

"He couldn't be unconscious somehow?" Sigrid whispered.

"No," said Giles slowly. "I don't think so. He's seen me before. If you will both move away for a moment I think I can handle it."

Sigrid nodded at the guard and they moved off down the corridor. Giles stooped to enter the low archway and walked up to the Dagda. Softly, he said first what he knew the old man wanted to hear.

"I gave orders upstairs that the others be allowed to rest. They're comfortable now."

With his eyes still closed, the Dagda slowly nodded. Giles saw the stiff posture of his body relax.

"I'll have to tell you the rest quickly, the guards are just down the hall. I have been to Earth."

It was the first time Giles had said the words aloud to anyone, and he felt a shock of affirmation. The Dagda didn't move or respond in any way. Drawing a deep breath, Giles continued.

"But I'm afraid something may have happened. Lir Regan was there and as we were talking one of the Watchers appeared. A girl named Sigrid whom I know. . . ." Giles paused. This explanation was difficult and there wasn't much time. "She was carrying a weapon and Lir Regan told me to run back to the globe. I did. I'm afraid she may have harmed your niece. I don't know."

He heard the footsteps of Sigrid and Duncan returning down the corridor and hurriedly whispered the rest. "She says she dreamed her journey to Earth but she could be lying. She might have discovered the lost fleet. The Head of the Watchers knows of Earth, or says he knows, and I know him. He's a vicious, unprincipled person, and he's given orders to use Judgments against your people. He wants you released in my custody now because he wants to find Lir Regan. . . ."

There wasn't time for more. Sigrid and Duncan were standing just outside the arch.

Still the Dagda didn't open his eyes. He said, in a voice so low that Giles had to strain to hear, "There are two hundred of us here."

"Not so many," Giles said gently. "Only about fifty."

"There are two hundred," the Dagda repeated. "Not just above where you saw them, but hidden below."

Giles felt a wild surge of elation. "Then they didn't find you all!"

"But almost all the children are among the fifty upstairs." The old man's words came very slowly, urgently. "And I want you to do something more. We must have a meeting up above. You must be there."

"I can't do that!" Giles whispered. "I can take you with me, but that's all the authority I have. I got away with the other order by pure luck."

"You will have to do more," the Dagda said. "I will not move until a meeting is called." His eyes remained closed and his breath came so slowly that it seemed it might stop altogether.

Giles whispered frantically, "I can't!" just as Sigrid came in beside him. The Dagda didn't move. Giles drew Sigrid out of the room and beckoned to Duncan. Then he walked a little way down the corridor with them.

"You have my authorization to take that man," he reminded the guard.

Duncan cast an uneasy glance back at the small room and nodded.

Giles looked at Sigrid, "And you are here to see that I don't make any—mistakes." He ignored her quick protest and continued. "The greatest mistake right now would be to ignore the order I'm about to give. We are going to let the Earth Worshippers have another meeting—right now."

Duncan began to protest but Sigrid was faster. "What kind of a game is this, Giles? Saunders warned me you might do something like this—" Startled at her own disclosure, she stopped.

So, it was out! She must have reported to Saunders, and she might well know she'd been on Earth. If she had harmed Lir Regan in any way, she wouldn't have told Saunders who wanted the girl, and needed Giles as a contact. They must both realize by now that he was playing a double game. It didn't matter. He would try to get the Dagda what he wanted. The old man wasn't a fool—there must be something in back of his demand.

"We are after a girl," Giles began, "who may be hidden here. There are so many guards about that there can't be any real trouble. But you can be sure if she is here, and there's a meeting, she'll appear regardless of our presence." Now, he wondered, what would Sigrid say?

Surprisingly, she agreed. "That's true. These people are all crazy and that girl especially would never think of the consequences. I'm sorry, Giles, it's a good idea."

His heart leaped with hope. If she wasn't lying, it meant Lir Regan was safe—somewhere.

"Do you think the old man will lead them?" she asked.

"I think it's the only way to get him out of that room."

She nodded, saying to Duncan, "Have your men ready for questioning in case she appears. And make whatever arrangements are necessary for the meeting. Green lights, anything. Give them what they want. We'll be up presently." He started to go and she added, "And do be ready for the other thing. Possibly Judgments will have to be immediate. Do you understand?"

Duncan nodded and left.

"I told Car Saunders about your contact with that girl," said Sigrid.

Giles waited. Was she now going to tell him about seeing Lir Regan and himself on Earth?

"The report I had on the way she spoke to you on the street that night," Sigrid added, "made me think she might reveal something important to you. We discovered you're one of the few people she's ever spoken to, other than real Earth Worshippers. Saunders always guessed she might be special, but we didn't know she was actually the keeper of the secrets. I hope this meeting works, Giles. He really wants that girl."

Giles stared at her. It all rang true. He wondered if Sigrid actually accepted him in this role of Watcher. . . .

She put her hand on his arm and smiled, but there was something hard, like a threat, in her eyes. "Giles— I just hope you don't want her, too."

He couldn't answer, but he managed to keep his expression steady. "I'd better get the old man now," he said, turning away.

The Dagda was still standing in that erect posture but his eyes were wide open and blazing—with a secret dream, Giles thought. What would he do with his meeting? Was it to be a last blessing of those about to come under Judgments—or could he inspire them to actual rebellion and revolt? He'd said others were hidden below. Giles wondered if they could fight their way to that fleet of ships. The Dagda must know where they were hidden. . . .

He wanted to ask where, and what he could do, but Sigrid was by his side.

"Come," the Dagda said, "I think they are waiting for us."

118

He bent under the arch and walked slowly to the steps, moving a little as if he were monarch of this underground kingdom.

Sigrid, after raising her brows at Giles, fell into a mock step behind. He wondered how this meeting would affect her, if it would reinforce her "dream" of Earth, or cause her to remember the reality. He was afraid of her and of what she might do, afraid of what might happen upstairs. But there was something in following that stately old man that freed him for a moment from his fear.

▓▓▓▓▓ ELEVEN ▓▓▓▓▓

Between us and the heavy temptations
Between us and the shame of the world
Between us and the death of captivity . . .

The children sat cross-legged in front of their elders looking up with round eyes at the Dagda as he led the chant. Behind them voices of their parents and all the Earth Worshippers rose and fell in rhythmic waves.

The green lights the Watchers had restored cast flickering shadows on the group of people sitting on the floor. Around them the black capes of the Watchers circled like a border of death . . . the death of captivity. . . .

The words of the song were heavy. The Dagda looked down at the children, and as if wishing to release them from the mysterious fear that echoed in their eyes, smiled and changed to a lighter invocation.

From every brownee and banshee. . . .

The children clapped their hands, laughing, and eagerly joined in.

From every nymph and water wraith
From every fairy mouse and grass mouse. . . .

It seemed to be their special song. Giles looked in wonder at their uplifted faces, listening to the high, light voices that rose above the rest. He tried to fit the words with the life they had known—a world of black cinders, ash, and soot. Could they know the meaning of grass, the magic of water? What associations could the words possibly have for them? Wouldn't they sing as eagerly about the dust of Niflhel?

From every troll among the hills . . .
Oh! Save me till the end of my day,
Oh! Save me till the end of my day.

Silently, Giles repeated the prayer . . . save them till the end of their day.

Beside him, Sigrid was watching with amusement. They stood at the end of the circle of guards, nearest the Dagda. Giles couldn't yet determine what the man intended to do. So far it had been a meeting like any other but confined to chants. The Dagda had not spoken of Earth. But he didn't need to. Earth was reflected in the eyes of each person along the floor. And Sigrid, too, Giles knew, was thinking of Earth. He wondered how she visualized it, how she visualized herself there. He wondered why she was amused; because they were waiting for nothing?

He wished he could disappear from this circle of guards and look for the others who were hidden below. But the Dagda had indicated to Giles before this meeting that he must remain. Whatever happened now was in the Dagda's hands.

An Tri numh
A chumhnadh
A chomhnadh . . .

It was the same strange chant he had heard before. Those odd words. The Dagda was saying them alone. His voice was deep and steady and clear and reached the farthest recess of the huge hall.

As if the words frightened her, Sigrid stiffened and held on to Giles's arm.

The sacred three
To save
To surround . . .

Giles started. The words had changed and the voice was changing. In back of the Dagda another clearer sound came ringing through the room, a feminine voice. Slowly the Dagda's voice faded away and there was only that bell-like tone . . .

The hearth
The house
The household . . .

Standing beside the Dagda, as if she had appeared from mist, was Lir Regan, her hands stretched out before her.

This eve, this night, O. This eve!

Sigrid gave a signal to the Watchers. Giles threw her arm aside and dashed for Lir Regan. The Dagda was standing close beside her. She reached out and drew Giles close, away from the guards. The voices of the Earth Worshippers rose in screams. Ash rose from the

floors in a blinding flurry . . . everyone had risen . . .
Giles felt it covering his hair, his eyes. . . . He rubbed
his knuckles against the lids quickly and opened his
eyes. . . .

And looked at Lir Regan.

They were standing on a grassy rising by the banks of
a small stream.

Everywhere the trees rose in infinite variety, rising
and spreading in graceful profusion. Low in the sky the
sun hung red, a flaming disk streaking the clouds with
pink and orange and gold. A light mist was settling
along the undergrowth, curling around grass and shrubs,
lifting in wispy tendrils about the trunks of trees. Somewhere in the distance there was an insistent rushing, a
rise and fall, a gentle thunder crashing and fading away.

Lir Regan was still holding his hand. Beside, the
Dagda had his arm linked through hers. Now she released them both and standing back, looked at Giles
with an odd, searching expression.

Suddenly he began to tremble. The hall at the Branxholm, the ash, the circle of guards, that cloud. . . .

Fearfully he stared at Lir Regan, unable to control his
panic. His mind tumbled in wild gyrations, and suddenly, irrationally, he wished to be away, to be
back. . . .

"Don't!" Lir Regan quickly put out her hand to
steady him. Holding his arm firmly she drew him down
to the grass and sat down beside him. "I'm sorry, Giles."
Her voice was sympathetic, light, and clear. The natural
sound of it helped him.

He continued to look at her while slowly, gradually,
his body stopped shaking and his heart resumed its nor-

mal beat. The Dagda, watching the scene guardedly, smiled and sat down beside them.

"There was no other way this time, Giles," said Lir Regan. Her green eyes reflected the light of the leaves.

Giles gazed back steadily and asked, "Was it you, then?"

"Yes, this time it was."

"And you. . . ." He stopped. He had no reference point. There were no words for what he wished to ask.

"I am only myself," Lir Regan softly answered his unspoken question. "I am exactly what you know of me— the Dagda's niece. And beyond that I am the Bard, yes."

"What you really wish to know is something different, Giles," the Dagda broke in. "But Lir Regan did bring us here this time, it's true."

"I couldn't stay," she said. "They would have caught me this time, and there is a limit."

"The others!" cried Giles suddenly, springing to his feet.

"Yes, you must go back. The time has come. That's why I brought you here, to tell you how, to show you the way." Lir Regan jumped to her feet, too, and spoke hurriedly. "There isn't too much time left, Giles, and you will have to do it. My uncle and I can't go back now."

"They've invoked Judgments for our people, Lir Regan," the Dagda said.

She looked at him with terror in her eyes. It was the first time Giles had seen her show fear.

"Then you must go now, Giles!" she cried.

"And all the children are in the main hall with those who were caught," the Dagda told her.

124

She stared and whispered, "The children—then is there time?"

"Perhaps—if he goes now," the Dagda urged. .

"But how?" asked Giles. "How can I return?"

Lir Regan turned to her uncle and he shook his head. There was still a question in her eyes as she looked at Giles, but making a sudden decision, she cried, "There isn't time to explain now. Just follow me!" and she began to run down the slope.

He caught up with her quickly and followed as she led him in a twisting path through the maze of trees, down to the stream and along its curving edge. The sun was sinking lower as they ran, bathing the earth in a red-gold twilight. Running through that golden mist with the droplets of water on the rocks reflecting like jewels, Giles felt they were running into the heart of the sun. . . .

"Follow me!" Lir Regan called again. And Giles, the sun in his eyes, in his mouth, in his hair, lighting him like a streak of gold, ran on.

TWELVE

Not much time had elapsed. The main hall was still foggy from that sudden shower of ash, the green globes flickered palely behind specks of soot in the air. Dirt was digging in under the doors through cracks in the old building. Outside, Giles heard gusts of wind buffeting the walls. The storm had reached the Branxholm —just as Lir Regan had said it would.

He shivered, wondering again at her knowledge, her strange powers. But there wasn't time to question—she had warned him not to try.

The Earth Worshippers were again lined up against the wall and all the Watcher guards were now inside the building. They stood with their weapons out and pointed at each man and woman. The children were whimpering with fear. Far across the hall a long table had been set up, and there was activity around it. Giles caught a glimpse of Sigrid's heavy blonde hair. Her hood was thrown back and she was speaking with a man. Giles squinted through the dim light. It looked like Car Saunders. So he was here! Giles wondered if he would be behind that table where chairs were being placed. They were obviously forming an impromptu "Court."

His heart began to race. Everything depended now on time, outer time, the time of the storm, and his own inner timing. The responsibility made him afraid. The palms of his hand were sweating. He was standing at the head of the steps that led to the underground caverns. He pulled his hood low to shield his face and slowly walked to the line of captive people. With so many guards about, they took no notice of him. They were more concerned with the darkening hall and the sounds outside. Something had gone wrong with their lighting system for there were no harsh spotlights, only the pale green globes, slowly fading.

Giles edged his way to the line of people, trying to find the man Arthur whom Lir Regan had described. Tall, thin, brown hair, a narrow, high-bridged nose— the same man who had assisted the Dagda at that first meeting. He might be standing with his two children, boys about five and six. Finally, at the far end of Earth Worshippers, Giles saw him. He waited until the man caught his eye, then quickly made the gesture Lir Regan had showed him. It was a simple movement; he merely clasped his hands together at his chest and swiftly dropped them.

Arthur, eyes fast on Giles, raised his head and softly cleared his throat. Giles smiled and made a quick nod. So much was easy—now they knew each other.

But the lights were growing brighter, and there was a lull in the wind outside. A Watcher whirled to glance at him curiously. Giles walked away to Sigrid and Car Saunders.

127

This was the moment he feared. If everything didn't come together at just the right time—Saunders saw him first and exclaimed in surprise.

Sigrid turned around, but before she had a chance to speak, Giles grabbed her arm. Pulling her closer to Saunders, he said in a low voice, "What did you do with them? Tell us where they are!"

"Just a minute, Giles," Saunders frowned.

"She has the Dagda and his niece, Saunders," Giles told him, holding Sigrid tightly.

"He's lying!" She tried to pull away. "Call a guard!"

"Wait!" Saunders's eyes were icy. "Explain this, Giles. I understood it another way."

"He ran for the girl and got them both away," Sigrid panted, wrenching her arm free.

"And you were right behind me," Giles accused. "I did run, and so did you, and the next thing I knew you were all gone."

Saunders watched the scene intently. His gaze moved from Sigrid's outraged expression to Giles's fury.

A sudden gust of wind rocked the old building, and again the lights began to dim. Giles didn't know how long he could keep this up, but if he guessed Saunders correctly, the suspicion he was throwing on Sigrid would be enough to occupy and delay him. . . .

The table was up, the chairs were set, the "Court" was ready. And there wasn't a true Magistrate about. Three men stood in back of that table, waiting for a signal from Saunders. He was obviously in charge. In back of all his other impressions, Giles realized he was seeing the true inner workings of Niflhel. Not the court of justice people believed in, but a mock court, run by the Society of Protectors.

128

"Don't start anything, Saunders," Giles warned him, "until she tells you where she hid the old man and the girl. There may be others—"

Wind whined along the floor, raising dirt that made their eyes smart. Only a little longer, thought Giles, blinking at Saunders who watched them both, frowning.

The wind began to pound upon the building in angry, savage blows. Suddenly, with no warning, the huge entrance doors blew open, and the storm raged into the Branxholm. Sigrid was almost knocked off her feet by the blinding rush of windswept dirt.

Giles caught his balance and shouted, "Watch her, Saunders!"

He saw Car Saunders reach out, stumbling, and then the hall became a nightmare. The lights went out completely. The Watcher guards were buffeted by the wind, tangled in their capes, slapped against each other—Lir Regan had been right! Now if only the man Arthur had kept his place.

Giles ran back, twisting and turning between the guards, rubbing his eyes—he was barely able to see the Earth Worshippers through the flying soot. Dimly he perceived Arthur holding to one child, and the little boy holding on to his brother. . . .

"We are all together," Arthur whispered.

And echoing Lir Regan's words, Giles said. "Follow me!" He took Arthur's hand.

In all that darkness, blinded by the dirt and wind, the Earth Worshippers were the only ones who managed to keep together, in place. Feeling his way in the dark, Giles led them toward the stairwell—and then he was frightened again. He could sense the Watchers behind them, floundering in the dark. But there were fifty people to lead down the stairs. . . . Inch by slow inch they made their way down to the level just below. And here it was not as safe as above, for the air wasn't yet black from the storm—here there was just a heavy grayness.

"Quickly!" Giles called over his shoulder, and heard echoes repeated along the line. He led them down, past the large chamber of their meetings to another corridor, and then past the low tunnel that led to the cave of the hangings. There, just beyond a sharp bend, Giles stopped to exchange places with Arthur. "You'll have to lead us from here," he whispered, "to the others."

Arthur nodded and placed his child's hand in Giles's. The line of people had all stopped—and now they listened. Faintly, they heard the sound of the storm still raging above. They couldn't tell yet if they were being followed. . . .

Arthur walked on swiftly, on and on down the corridor, and then finally stopped. Everyone in back stopped again. In the silence they could hear feet running somewhere above and behind.

It was like another nightmare. Giles wanted to push Arthur, to hurry him, but he was moving his hand very slowly over the rough rocks. His little boy's hand, in Giles's, squeezed tightly. It was like a warning to be patient.

Arthur's hand stopped on a segment of rock that jutted out in an almost imperceptible wedge. He first put his ear against it, then, with maddening slowness, knocked four times.

One of the children in the line started to cry. Giles heard the mother hush it. Arthur knocked four times again. Then, inch by slow inch, the rock began to move aside. A whole part of the hewn-out corridor opened to reveal another cave room. Arthur and Giles stood aside, urging the people in. In back, down the corridor, they could now hear voices.

"Hurry, hurry!" they whispered, pushing the people through.

It seemed years before the last person entered and at last Giles and Arthur followed them. And again they waited for the heavy rock to close behind them.

The group huddled together, mothers with their arms around their children, hands over mouths. Outside they heard feet running by. No one breathed until those footsteps returned, and they heard shouts as the Watchers ran back the other way.

Arthur stood by the wall, his fingers to his lips, warning the children. "They may have left someone outside to watch this part of the caves," he whispered. "So we must all be very, very quiet. Now come quickly, and we will go to the others."

Only the one man who had let them in was in this small cavern. On one side was a narrow, slanting tunnel, leading deeper down into the rocks of Niflhel. Giles breathed freely at last. It couldn't be far now. He took up the end of the line, and picked up a little girl who was stumbling, too tired to walk. She clung gratefully to him, and putting her arms around his neck, fell fast asleep. Giles smiled down at her, wondering what kind of an awakening she would have. If Lir Regan was right. . . .

But he didn't dare hope for that. It would be too much of a miracle. He couldn't yet believe it.

They followed the tunnel down, deeper and deeper, and finally came out in the complex of caverns where the Earth Worshippers had been hidden. Quietly, wearily, the group sank down to rest while the others rushed to make them comfortable with pillows and blankets and food.

Giles looked around in amazement. He had been prepared for another large cave like the one on the first level, but this was more like a small city. His eyes followed the large central hall to a group of smaller rooms leading off it, with equipment for storage and cooking, dormitories for sleeping. Arthur came to sit beside him after settling his children down to rest. He smiled at Giles's open surprise.

"Some of us have lived down here for years," he said. "Those that the Society particularly wanted to Classify —as individuals. They've never tried to use mass Judgments before, though. When we had some warning we just quietly disappeared, down here."

"So I was right," Giles murmured. "Lir Regan didn't have time to explain everything, but I guessed the Society, and maybe the government, was at fault."

"It's the Society," said Arthur. "Some of the men in government are excellent people and have no idea what's going on. But others are very close to the Society and take their orders from them. 'Protectors!' " Arthur laughed shortly.

"And Car Saunders?"

"Has unlimited power," Arthur replied seriously. "He wants to get rid of those who know too much. He, and some others in the Society suspect the existence of Earth."

132

"They know it's real, don't they?" asked Giles.

"No. They're not sure," said Arthur. "Many of our own people don't know their dream is a reality. They think of Earth as a legend from the past, or a religion. They simply wish to be free to worship. I've worked with the Dagda for years and we've tried to prepare a few—only a few—for the reality."

Giles nodded, looking over the many faces, each so different. "Yes, you'd have to be careful. And how many have actually been to Earth?"

There was no answer.

Surprised, Giles looked at the man beside him. He was staring at Giles with a strange expression in his intelligent eyes; what was it? Startled, incredulous, yearning, wary, all at once. Giles felt a shock inside.

"How many, Arthur?" he repeated gently.

Unexpectedly, the man's eyes filled with tears. "You don't mean that you. . . ?" The question was left unfinished while Giles slowly nodded.

He felt himself shrink under Arthur's scrutiny. Wondering why he felt so ashamed, he nodded again. He didn't have to repeat his question. But why had *he* been the only one? The question bothered him terribly until he remembered what Lir Regan had said; it had to be someone who was opposed to the idea. Someone who didn't believe in Earth. But he still didn't understand, and couldn't shake off his feeling of shame. He looked at the people around him who had spent their lives worshipping a dream; he couldn't reconcile the irony of having been the only one. . . .

Nervously, he rose to his feet. Lir Regan said that *time* was important—they had limited time. He cared about nothing now except trying to help these people reach a place they didn't even know existed.

"Have they rested enough?" he asked Arthur. "I think we must be on our way."

Still with that odd look, Arthur stood up beside him. "On our way?" he repeated, his voice numb.

Giles felt his own position, with this man, as an embarrassment. "In Lir Regan's and the Dagda's absence," he said, "you are the leader. You must help me. Lir Regan asked me to show you this. She said you would understand."

Giles reached into an inner pocket where he had concealed the tiny thing she had given him. He put it on the palm of his hand and held it out to Arthur.

The man began to reach for it, and then pulled back his hand as if he'd been stung. He stood very quietly, without touching it, and looked at it for a long time. Finally Arthur nodded, and with a look of such burning hope that it frightened Giles, and softly, "I will help. Please lead us on our way."

Giles closed his hand and put the blade of grass back in his inner pocket.

THIRTEEN

The Dagda and Lir Regan were waiting for them. She stood beside a large boulder, her white gown blowing softly in the warm night under the stars.

Maybe, Giles thought, it was a blessing that it was night. He didn't know how many in this large group of people might have reacted too strongly, even fallen, under the impact of Earth in the day. As it was, they would have a gradual dawn to help them face the new splendor of the sun.

The night was beautiful enough for a beginning. Almost too beautiful, he thought, seeing them sink to the ground one by one. They looked up at the blazing stars with awe-filled eyes that opened and closed and opened again; they were unable to take it in all at once. Giles had wondered how it would be, shouts and cries of joy, weeping—hysteria, perhaps? He was totally unprepared for this uncanny silence. There wasn't a whisper other than the whisper of wind among the trees.

They came out in a worshipful silence, so quiet there was only the rise and fall of their breathing. Giles thought he could hear heartbeats. They sank down on the ground under the stars and laid their children down carefully on beds of grass under the cover of the soft night wind. It was so still. . . .

The children slept quietly, their small faces upturned to the sky. Here and there an older child was awake, lips parted, eyes roving across the stars nestling in the dark bed of the sky. Hands hesitantly fingered the grass, stroked the ground, heads bowed to rub against the body of the Earth . . . and no one spoke.

It was so still. . . .

Lir Regan came to lead Giles away. The moon lighted a path for them. She took him well away from the others into a small clearing surrounded by trees. The Dagda was waiting, and when he saw Giles, came up to take both his hands. "Thank you!"

"No, I'm ashamed," Giles replied. "It should have been your Arthur."

Smiling, the Dagda shook his head. "It doesn't matter. They're all here now."

"And you're sure they can't find us?" Giles turned to Lir Regan doubtfully. There was so much he didn't understand; it still seemed like a dream.

"Yes, I'm sure," she said, "but you're not, are you? You don't know why they can't find us, why they never will."

"No," Giles shook his head. He didn't know. She had said there was no fleet of ships, only one green globe, but still he didn't understand. She had sent him back to Niflhel with her strange power, but told him that she couldn't bring so many to Earth in quite the same way. She had told him to find Arthur and to lead the people down that long, dark tunnel. He had found it, and then with Arthur's help, led the way. At each step he had faltered, unable to believe that there wasn't a fleet of hidden ships, feeling that he was leading them to nothing—deeper and deeper into nothing—into the rocks of Niflhel. Behind him were two hundred exhausted people, patiently following, hoping. He had gone on through that endless tunnel, finding beyond each bend . . . nothing—no globes, no miracles, nothing but an ever-deepening darkness. And yet they had kept following.

She had said he would lead them to Earth, and he had. For finally, when he had given up all hope, when he wanted to turn back, he had gone on past one last bend. And there, like a mirage at the end of endless darkness, was a night filled with stars, and a fresh wind blowing down the tunnel, and Lir Regan waiting in her white gown.

"No, I don't understand," Giles repeated. If they had come like this, why couldn't all of Niflhel?

And where had they come? Where were they? Where was Niflhel? A man couldn't walk to Earth—walk to another planet through a tunnel underground—or a tunnel in the sky?

"Giles," Lir Regan said softly, "you remember that girl who appeared on Earth—that Watcher who almost saw you here. . . ."

It made Giles sick to hear Lir Regan speak of Sigrid now. It reminded him too much of what had been. There was even a sorrow about Sigrid—a wish that none of it had been the way it was. He didn't want to be reminded now, not on Earth, not from Lir Regan.

But she said, "You have to know sometime, Giles. The reason that girl appeared on Earth was not because she'd found another globe—there isn't any. Nor did she find a fleet of ships—there isn't a fleet. She came to Earth because I had been thinking very strongly about her. And you and I had just been speaking about the homecoming of man to Earth. Do you remember?"

Giles nodded.

"We had both agreed that all men must not come home, that all were not ready. And after that I was thinking about Sigrid—yes, I know her name. I shouldn't have been, but for a moment I wondered if you would possibly want her here. Because of your past together, because you might feel sorry. And I wondered so strongly, Giles, that for a moment she was here on Earth. It was my fault. An accident. I was afraid she might see you. There would have been a great danger if she had."

Appeared on Earth . . . Giles remembered that twice or more he had thought Lir Regan appeared, in the Underground, in front of the hanging.

"But Sigrid isn't you," he protested. "I know you have some strange power, Lir Regan, but Sigrid doesn't. She can't just appear."

"Can't she?" asked Lir Regan. "Right now, at this very moment, anything can appear, Giles. Not only Sigrid, but anything in Niflhel. Niflhel can appear. I'll show you."

"Regan!" the Dagda remonstrated quickly, but she shook her head.

"No, he must see for himself."

"It's dangerous," the old man argued.

"Look, Giles, if you want to see Niflhel, or if you want to be in Niflhel—" She took his hand.

And the woodland glade vanished.

138

They were standing on a street, the last fury of the soot storm dying around them. The factories belched their red flames in the eastern sky, and in the distance the huts were covered with blankets of ash, blacker than ever from the storm.

"No! Lir Regan!" Giles protested, shivering with fear. Two black-caped figures were approaching from up the street.

The men stopped for a moment in obvious disbelief of Lir Regan's white dress, and then began running toward them.

"Hold me," she whispered, "and think of Earth strongly, Giles, strongly!"

Still the men came running and nothing happened. Lir Regan became very quiet. She closed her eyes and her touch on Giles's arm was like a feather.

The Dagda rose out of the soot which slowly vanished along with the street of Niflhel, and they were back in the glade on Earth.

"You will not do that again!" the old man said. His voice was stern and reproachful.

"No," Lir Regan opened her eyes and brushed off her dress. "It won't be necessary. Giles has seen what he has to."

"And what the others must never see!" the Dagda's words were a command. "Or know is possible until the way is closed again." He looked at Giles closely, and was satisfied.

As if her job was finished, Lir Regan sat down on the grass and looked off in the distance. But Giles stood before her and his voice, in the still night, demanded an answer.

"Lir Regan," he said, "where are we?"

"On Earth." The tone of her voice, rising at the end, made the whole thing seem perfectly natural.

"And where is Niflhel?" Giles insisted.

"On Earth," she repeated quietly.

Shaken, Giles looked around. He looked up at the stars twinkling overhead, he felt the grass beneath his feet, he smelled the air . . . no, it was fantastic, he thought, impossible.

But the Dagda nodded. "Yes, Giles, Niflhel is all around you, just as Earth is around Niflhel, but out of reach. The ancient ones had a name for it—in their language it was called parallel worlds, but that does not give the right understanding. In that sense Niflhel is another planet. But in another, much truer sense, we are there now, as Niflhel is here."

He watched Giles for a moment and said gently, "Sit down and I will try to explain."

Lir Regan nodded at her uncle gratefully. "I had better get back to the others." She smiled at Giles and pressed his hand before she left the clearing.

"My niece is tired," the Dagda said. "This is much harder for her than appears." He was still looking closely at Giles.

And sitting on the grass, Giles wondered if everything he had experienced would suddenly be shattered. Was he in the middle of a dream? He didn't understand what the old man had said. Did it mean that at any moment they might find themselves back in that world of death, in Niflhel?

"Once in the caves," Giles murmured, "you said you would explain; you told me about Earth."

"Yes," said the Dagda. "And now I will tell you about Niflhel."

FOURTEEN

"You had the idea that man had escaped to Niflhel," the Dagda smiled. "And you felt, quite naturally, that man had escaped in ships of some kind to another planet. Well, we couldn't tell you everything then."

He looked up at the bright stars in the clear night sky, and said, his voice heavy, "Can you imagine what man had to become to lose all this?"

He paused for a moment and Giles felt there was a kind of prayer going on inside him. Then he continued. "I told you truthfully about the great horror, the monstrous conflagration that struck Earth. What led up to it, how it happened, we don't know. The scientists and those they took with them into the caves made sure we would never know."

"Caves? But you said ships, stars."

"No, I didn't say it," the Dagda's voice was patient. "But you thought it. It's a natural thought and a good one. Thanks to that thought we needn't fear those left on Niflhel who would like to find us—not that they could.

"No, Giles, there were no ships, no stars, there wasn't time. We know that. Apparently their science and technology was concerned with something quite different, something that harmed both themselves and their world. There was death on the face of the Earth, so they escaped underground into the caves they had prepared. The same caves you have just left—the caves under Niflhel. They were prepared to wait there for centuries, if necessary, until they could emerge again.

"And when they went underground they left behind to be destroyed all their secrets of power and technology. They left behind their records of flight, records of weaponry, records of political science.

"Do you know what they did take with them, Giles? Can you guess? It will answer many of your questions about the Earth Worshippers."

Mutely, Giles shook his head.

The Dagda smiled. "They took with them only their great myths, legends, epic poems, their Bibles and various religious books and their music!

"Outside of what was absolutely essential for life underground everything was left to be destroyed in the flames. The scientists had turned violently against their own technology. They hoped that man, by seeking the truths hidden in the old legends, could fashion a better world than that he had left."

Giles leaned forward intently, hanging on every word. There was something in what the Dagda was saying that filled him with mixed emotions of joy and shame. He couldn't separate from the feeling that he, too, was part of this ancient story, that it somehow involved him in a direct and personal way.

"They had thought in the beginning of their life underground that all men felt the same, that all wished the same, that when at last Earth was free from the forces that made her unfit for life, they would come out together and in the same hope begin anew.

"But the new evil began again under the rocks even before the last evil was finished. Men again split into different camps, with different ideas, and unfortunately this happened before the memory of certain technologies had been lost. Those who remembered began seeking power again, and the books of the great myths and poetry, and the Bibles, passed secretly into the hands of those who kept the original dream.

"And right there, in the caves under Niflhel, the civilization of Niflhel started long before man ever walked up from under the ground."

"The Examination!" cried Giles. "The history of Niflhel!"

"Yes," the Dagda quoted the words Giles had said three years ago. " 'Man had his beginning in the rock under Niflhel.' The history that you studied is, in a way, quite true."

"But there was something wrong," Giles said, remembering how he had felt a lie in the words.

"Yes, you are told only half the story. Fortunately, not many people know the other half. The people who say they know of Earth, like Car Saunders, only suspect. They wish it to be true. And they will keep looking for that fleet of ships until the end of time and never find it—because it doesn't exist."

"But the globe!" Giles remembered with sudden fear. "They could find the globe."

143

"No," the Dagda shook his head. "They won't find the globe. It was made by one of the early scientists who was loyal to the dream of Earth, and who was himself a Bard. He made it when the trouble first began, as a means of crossing the invisible barrier between our worlds.

"You see, Giles, always, since the time when men first disagreed, there has been a Bard. The books had to be hidden, the ideas protected somehow. The great traditions and legends were all that was left for man. It explains why all men now are called, at least partly, after the names of those in the ancient stories. Our first generations knew no other names.

"At first, being keepers of the books, the Bards only served the function of reading and reciting to those who met to keep the idea of Earth alive."

Giles was reminded, shamefully, of how those words had first affected him.

"In that way," the Dagda said, "they became the leaders of those who dreamed of Earth. And then slowly, through the centuries, as the Bards schooled themselves more and more in the great words, they began to unlock some of the secrets hidden within.

"At one time on Earth, the Bards, particularly the Druidic Bards, were thought to have magical powers, invisible forces at their command. And under the rocks of Earth-Niflhel, the new Bards came slowly to understand that power. For centuries they had used the globe as a means of seeing Earth. But at last they were able themselves to cross the barrier between worlds without aid. The globe was no longer needed for that purpose, but it was kept for another. It was kept for your use."

Giles stared at the Dagda who smiled patiently.

"Oh, yes, Giles. We didn't know who you would be, but your help was foretold long ago, when it was first understood by the Bards that one day man could come home. Lir Regan recognized you when that time came."

The Dagda raised his hand. "Do not ask me how, Giles. I was the previous Bard but I am old now, and Lir Regan is the keeper of the secrets. I do know that when man is safely home again the globe will destroy itself. No one on Niflhel will find it."

"But there is the tunnel," said Giles.

"Yes, the tunnel is open again," the old man said thoughtfully, "for a time, for those who can find it. The same tunnel through which man came to Niflhel so many centuries ago. It leads in both directions.

"Can you see that ancient journey, Giles? Can you see that group of men and women after thousands of years underground, coming up at last to meet that flat, ash-strewn planet devoid of life—or any reason for life. A planet habitable only because the atmosphere, foul as it was, could sustain life—shortened lives. Can you imagine what they saw?"

"Thousands of years, . . ." Giles murmured.

"They had raised generations underground. Generations of people who began to resemble, ever more closely and subtly, in their minds and hearts, the scene that greeted them when they finally climbed out. A barren land to support a barren people. I don't think they could have been surprised at what they saw. I think they must have recognized what they created."

Giles was very quiet. This could not be the answer . . . and yet he knew that it was.

145

"On Niflhel, Giles, they met the Earth they had created within themselves. They met their own inner environment. And beyond that, but hidden where they could never see it, lay the fair green land they had ruined."

Giles hardly breathed. "The land," he whispered, "the Earth, it can't. . . ."

"We don't know the intelligence or consciousness of Earth," said the Dagda firmly. "She may be capable of many disguises. There may be many Earths. Niflhel is as real as this. And yet we are here, on an Earth that had either accepted us, or an Earth reborn, or an Earth that has always been waiting.

"When man emerged from the rocks, he met Niflhel because Niflhel is what he was. He couldn't see beyond that screen to a different Earth. He met what he had to meet. He met himself when he met Niflhel."

"Niflhel," Giles said slowly.

"Yes. Without knowing it our ancestors named their new world correctly. It is an old, mythological name for Hell."

Giles raised his eyes to the stars. They were dimming now in the first pale hint of dawn.

"And that's exactly what they proceeded to make of it," said the Dagda softly. "The faults of their civilization had grown in them until they instinctively imitated what they'd left behind. Each step they took grew worse and worse. And as they became increasingly lost, Earth must have kept pace, removing herself ever further from their consciousness.

"Perhaps there's something in the Earth," the Dagda said slowly, "that will reject, at a certain point, what is

146

harmful to her. What mis-serves her purposes. Certainly man did not serve her well. And in misusing her he lost the possibility of serving himself. Remember that even the Earth Worshippers, those who dreamed and prayed, had to meet Niflhel as well. Perhaps Earth required that they, too, pay for something.

"It has been a long time since we had an opportunity like this."

"Like this—" said Giles.

"Yes," the Dagda paused for a long moment and then whispered, "Can you feel it?"

The air was very still. The wind might have been resting. The grass was damp and pungent, almost speaking to them with its smell. A faint pink light was beginning to creep over the horizon; Giles could see it through the trees. They stood with dark limbs outlined in the early dawn, stretching ever out and up, each leaf perfectly motionless. Giles looked at them in wonder, with a feeling of mystery. Were the trees waiting, guarding, praying? Yes, there was a guarded quality about all of Earth, a prayer in her waiting. Having accepted man again, was she so sure now? Why was it so still, so hushed, as if all life were in suspension, waiting. To see what man would do? To see what man could be?

Giles rose slowly, feeling as if the very touch of his feet on Earth was felt by her acutely as she waited. . . . It was as if Earth were holding her breath.

"Come," said the Dagda softly. "Dawn is breaking and the people will be waking and Earth is waiting to see."

147

FIFTEEN

It was the young child of Arthur that Giles saw first. The little boy of five. He was curled on the grass, cheek against an outflung arm, lips parted in sleep, eyelids moving slightly at the first stirrings of awakening. He moved on the grass, then stretched and blinked as his eyes slowly opened on the dawn. He was lying on his side, and as he began to take in the world around him, he first saw the grass and rubbed his hand carefully over the top of it. Then he brushed his cheek against it, and put his nose down and smelled it, and then he sat up, eyes wide open, to look at the sky.

He sat without moving while the sun rose, sending first shafts of gold, pillars of pink and orange, and then slowly climbed in a burst of radiance that showered the Earth with warmth.

Arthur's child watched it first with wide eyes, open mouth, and then as it rose ever higher, he stood up and took a few steps toward it, holding up his hands as if he could catch some of that lovely fire. He began to smile, and then to laugh, and then to run faster and faster toward the golden ball in the sky.

And with him the other children began to run; they were all awake, all tumbling and rushing and dancing down the slope, reaching up to that shining delight.

At the foot of the slope there was a shallow stream, bubbling and tumbling, running as quickly and lightly as the children. It seemed to come awake for them. And as if they all knew that catching the sun was a game, the children, in one graceful, harmonious movement, all discarded their clothes and tumbled in, laughing, splashing, singing, making fountains and waterfalls, making the stream grow with their play until it rose in wild sprays of color and sprinkled them with glistening, sparkling rainbow drops.

The adults silently watched the children.

Giles felt this was how it had to be. Whatever they were thinking and feeling under those overwhelming new impressions, the children were instinctively first to make friends with the Earth.

Yet away from that splash of life in the stream, Earth was still very quiet. There was not yet the murmur of life he had once heard himself.

Lir Regan waited quietly at the top of the slope, as if she could do no more, and yet as if something waited to be done. The Dagda waited beside her—as Earth was waiting. Giles held his breath. There was a focus of quiet, a center of silence more quiet than that of Earth.

It came from the group of people watching the children—was it up to them, then? What must they do? What was wanted of them?

With a flash of understanding, Giles felt he knew. Earth would accept these people, would accept man again, if they could accept her life. But after half-living in a world of death for so long, could they learn to live

149

again—or would they always be looking back, toward what they'd left in Niflhel? If they couldn't meet this demand of life, once again Earth would die.

Until now this had been a dream for them. It was easy to worship a dream, to fantasize a loveliness where all might be well. They couldn't have known, until now, that in return for her life, her reality, Earth would demand a real life from them. This time she would not accept half-men, half-women, who would not make that effort. And Giles felt that with every part of her being— with that intelligence and consciousness the Dagda had mentioned—Earth, because she wished for men, was straining for their understanding.

If they were not prepared to make this effort, Giles felt there would only be Niflhel—or worse. Yes, it could be even worse for these people who were so close to understanding, who had dreamed so long.

He walked up to join Lir Regan and the Dagda where they waited, still feeling that focus of silence from the people and the guarded quality about the Earth.

And then, very slowly, the group turned away from the children and looked up to where they were standing.

At the top of the slope was an open clearing surrounded by trees with one huge, gnarled ancient in the center.

One by one the people started to come up, as if they were pulled, none looking at the other, each intent on some private effort, some individual question. But together, as if it were understood, they grouped themselves around the great tree and sat down in a circle.

Hundreds of thousands of years ago man had done the same. Now he repeated the ancient ritual. Lir Regan

150

made her way to the front of the tree—so old that it could have had memories itself of the last Bard who had stood there.

The children, seeing their parents in the clearing, left their play in the stream, and came up to sit like solemn little plants in front of their elders. They clasped their small hands together hopefully, and Giles, watching them, felt a wish arise that was harder and stronger and fiercer than anything he'd ever known.

Softly, Lir Regan began her song.

She began it in a quiet on Earth that was beyond imagining.

I am a wind of the sea . . .
I am a stag of seven times . . .
I am a hawk on the cliff . . .
I am a tear of the sun . . .

Each time the group responded.

for depth . . .
for strength . . .
for deftness . . .
for clearness . . .

The song, if it was a song—it was more of a prayer—went on. And later, when it was finished, Lir Regan told an old legend. Giles heard only part of it, because he was listening so intently for what he thought was a whisper from Earth.

"And when the seven Bards were gathered," Lir Regan recited, "Catwg put to them seven questions.

" 'The greatest wisdom of man; what is that?'

"Replied one, 'The ability to do evil and not to do it.'

151

" 'The worst principle of man; what is that?'

" 'Falsehood,' came the answer from Taliesin, Chief of the Bards.

" 'And the greatest folly of man?'

"Ystyvan answered, 'To wish a common evil which he cannot do.'

" 'What is the noblest action of man?' said Catwg.

"And the son of Clydno Eddin, called Cynan, replied, 'Correcting.' "

Giles held his breath, listening, feeling—was it a touch of wind?

Lir Regan had started singing again.

> I am fair among flowers . . .
> I am a lake on a plain . . .
> I am a hill of poetry . . .

And everyone had joined her singing. Giles looked at them—they were suddenly robust, strong, and free. Their faces glowed. He thought they might not have known Earth before this minute. They sang strongly, loudly, joyfully, and the children were not solemn any more; they were up and lively and dancing in the clearing.

And they all felt the wind—all heard the voices of Earth—when she decided to speak. The trees rustled and leaves fluttered and birds appeared suddenly, flashing through the air in blue and scarlet streaks, chirping and singing, while below, in the grass, the murmur of small things began.

And from a cloudless sky, from a clear blue heaven, they were given the miracle of rain. It fell softly on their upturned faces, on hands held high to catch the golden, glistening drops. They stood bareheaded in the wetness, letting the rain wash them, smelling the damp perfume of ground and grass and flower and shrub. It seemed that Earth intensified herself in a gladness of their understanding.

Man had come home at last.

Later, after the incredible day that had belonged to the children, Giles and Lir Regan stood by the large boulder at the tunnel entrance. There would always be someone here now, to wait. Giles's last questions had been answered. He knew that no one on the other side could come this way unless they were prepared. They need not fear anyone on Niflhel because those they feared would never find the way. It was not for those people on Niflhel who sought death. It was for those who felt that somewhere a real life might exist. And when there was no one left to seek the way, the tunnel would close again.

Giles smiled at Lir Regan and took her hand. They had left Niflhel behind at last—and yet. . . .

All day he had been feeling it. Once he had thought Earth was the final answer, this coming home, the solution. But a new understanding stirred within him as he realized there was yet another home that he and all the rest must come to. It lay somewhere deep within him, and upon how well he and everyone understood it, would depend the future.

He looked up at the sky wondering how it was that having come home, man must now go on. Earth was only the beginning.

He whispered to Lir Regan, "I wonder what Earth

153

wants from us—and for us—and what she wants for herself?"

"I don't know," said Lir Regan softly. "That is the ultimate mystery. I've helped only to bring us this far. Now we must help each other find out."

The night was blazing with stars reaching into infinity. Giles knelt beside the boulder and looked down from that splendor in the sky to the long dark tunnel. The first to come home, he must now be the first to wait.

And as he waited and watched he thought he saw a vision of someone in the darkness. And he felt himself as a child again. He knew it was only his wish, his desire to thank her—for hadn't she given him the dream he didn't even know he carried—so long ago? Hadn't she secretly known and hoped?

He said the words silently in his heart, hoping that somewhere in some far place, she would hear.

"We have been standing in the rain, Grandmother!" he said to the memory of that gray-haired figure who had held her hands high in defiance of the soot of Niflhel.

"On Earth, we have been standing in the rain!"